A COLLECTION OF HEAVY METAL® GALLERIES

RELOAD:
A COLLECTION OF HEAVY METAL® GALLERIES

ISBN: 1-932413-25-1

Published by HEAVY METAL®
100 North Village Avenue, Suite 12
Rockville Centre, NY 11570

© 2005 Metal Mammoth, Inc.

All Rights Reserved under International and Pan-American Copyright Conventions.
The reproduction of this book in any form, electronic or mechanical, by any means
now known or hereafter invented including photocopy, recording, or by any information
storage and retrieval system, is expressly forbidden without written permission from the publisher.

All illustrations are Copyrighted © by the individual artists

Cover by Christopher J. Franchi

Cover concept by Robert V. Conte

Layout and Design by Gary Esposito for Chikara Entertainment, Inc.

Visit our website at www.heavymetal.com

First Printing: June 2005
10 9 8 7 6 5 4 3 2 1

Printed in China by Regent Publishing Services Limited.
Contact RegentNY2@aol.com for additional information.

THE TALENT:

RICHARD CORBEN
DANIEL TORRES
DOVILIO BRERO
PETER KUPER
LES EDWARDS
JULIE BELL
ARTHUR SUYDAM
SIMON BISLEY
GIL BRUVEL
TAYYAR OZKAN
ROB PRIOR
DORIAN CLEAVENGER
DAVID BOLLT
CLAUDIO ABOY
JOHN ZELEZNIK
LUIS ROYO
DAVID HO
MICHAEL WARD
JUSTICE HOWARD
MIKE DeWEESE
MYKE MALDONADO
LORENZO SPERLONGA
DREW POSADA
BRIAN ROOD
SCOTT BURTON
CIRUELO CABRAL
BORIS VALLEJO
JOHN SEVERIN
KEVIN EASTMAN
LIAM SHARP
KEN KELLY
MARK MORENO
CARLOS DIEZ
LAWRENCE NORTHEY
JASON FREENY
FELIX VEGA
KEN MEYER JR.
ANTHONY A PALUZZI
EDGAR ESPINO
VICTORIA FRANCES

INTRODUCTION

This book is dedicated to the memory of our dear friend, Bill Liebowitz (1941-2004), who believed, like all of us here at Heavy Metal, that it's all about the art! Some days I think Heavy Metal is at the center of it. I know it isn't true, but when I'm working with Howard on an upcoming issue, I often feel incredibly lucky, more than lucky, that so many AMAZING artists submit concepts and finished work to us each month.

It can also be heartbreaking, of course. I have to decide whose art will appear immediately and whose will appear later, even though I wish I could make each issue a 1000 pages and get ALL of the art we receive out sooner—the artwork that I've always been so passionate about, that has inspired me and so many others for over twenty eight years. I want you to be able to see it, love it, and hold it in your hands RIGHT NOW! But as I put each issue together, I always have to wait another month (or more) to get every story, or the next installment of a multi-part story, out to the fans who I know will totally freak on it.

Waiting is the hardest part, and we're all in the same boat. As hard as it is, we all know we can wait because the art is worth waiting for. After all, it really is all about the art, and I have known this from the start. When I began reading Heavy Metal in the late 70s, I often had no clue what the stories were about, and I could not have cared less. I loved the ART. It moved me, and that was enough. Even today, I publish art stories, and the writing is—well—puzzling, but I can live with it because the ART is so amazingly beautiful!

But I am digressing. What I really want to tell you about is this book, which features art that has appeared in Heavy Metal's Gallery over the years. The four-page Gallery first appeared in the early eighties and has been one of the most popular sections of the magazine ever since. I loved it when I was a reader, and when I bought the magazine, I regarded it as a feature that Heavy Metal could not do without. Finding NEW TALENT who couldn't wait to have their art featured in it has been way too easy—the hard part, as I said above, has been trying to get all the work out to you as quickly as possible. Now I at least get to put it out simultaneously.

Howard and I came up with the idea for a book devoted to the Gallery when we were thinking about publishing the 25th Anniversary Cover Book. We didn't think it would be possible to release two books together. Putting together a Gallery book, we knew, would be a long process because we would have to get permission from the artists to republish their work, and we hadn't heard from many of them in a long time. The book, we believed, would be incomplete if we didn't include all of their work. Unfortunately, we couldn't do that, but we did the best we could. We sent letter after letter—we found everyone we could find. The result is this superb collection of beautiful artworks by talented artists. These artists, some of whose work has also graced the covers or feature-artist section of Heavy Metal over the years, have all affected me in some way or another with their submission(s), and I felt honored to put their works in the Gallery. I feel even more honored to be able to reprint them now.

So, without taking up more space than I should (as I usually do), I'm going to bow to those who deserve all the credit for making such a killer book possible and for taking the "DREAM BY THE HORNS" and doing what it takes to get their artistic vision out there.

I also want to thank you for enjoying the artists of Heavy Metal as much as I do.

It's all about the art.

Kevin Eastman
Los Angeles, 2004

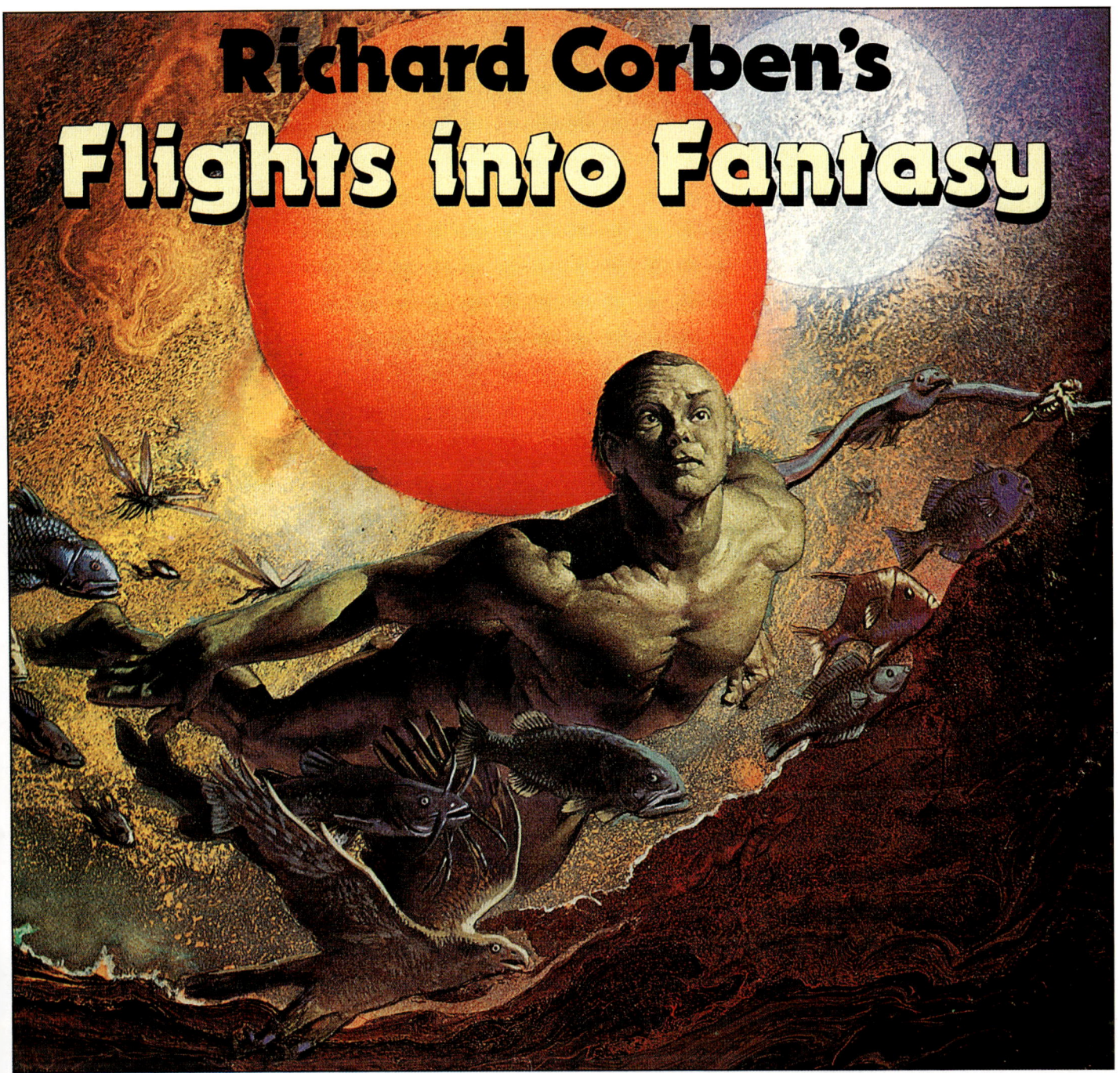

Gallery: Richard Corben's Flights into Fantasy

by Pete Hamill

In the late 1960s, the work of Richard Corben found its way out of Kansas City into the rest of America and then the world. From the beginning, it was clear that Corben was an American popular artist whose energy, power, and originality equaled those other children of Kansas City, Count Basie and Charlie Parker. Each had a unique vision, a way of seeing the world through a medium that had been dismissed as common and vulgar; Basie made swing music sound as fresh as a mountain stream; Charlie Parker could make you believe that nobody in history had ever played a saxophone. Corben took the comic strip, a form that seemed exhausted or in slick decay, and he seemed to reinvent the form.

Now there is a book—*Flights into Fantasy*—that tells us something about how Corben came to be Corben. I say "something." No book can tell us everything about a great artist, and I think Corben is a great artist.

The art in this Gallery section is from *Flights into Fantasy*, by Fershid Bharucha. All art is © 1981, by Richard V. Corben.

Obviously, his draftsmanship is powerful and original, but that is not why he is great. His squat, muscle-laced men do not exist in life; his voluptuous women are products of his imagination, not the gene pool; when they come together to make love, we don't observe delicate brief encounters so much as violent collisions, primitive needs sated in dense, thick receptions and penetrations. Corben has created in the tale of Den, his masterwork, visual metaphors for fucking. Not love-making. Fucking. You do not experience such extraordinary couplings in a world fashioned by Henry James or Henry Miller or even in the fevered pages of the skin magazines. Corben's power, the sheer lust of his imagination, demands its own world, and he has created that world. For me, the ability to invent an alternate world is the absolute mark of a great artist.

In this book, we can trace influences on Corben's work: just as Lester Young pointed the way for Charlie Parker, Will Eisner showed Corben the possibility of the comic book page. Panels shift in size and scale, figures burst out of perspective or recede into vast, barren distances. Eisner taught everybody in comics how to use sound, and Corben has built on Eisner's use of lettering to express inexpressible sound. He has also made short films that not many people have seen, but we don't need to experience Corben in a theater; he has frozen on the pages of books and magazines some of the most remarkable movies of the era. He has taken us to Neverwhere.

Corben also learned from others: Harvey Kurtzman, Frank Frazetta, Neal Adams, Jim Steranko, and the terribly undervalued Alex Toth; he absorbed what there was to learn from Wally Wood and Jack Davis. But Corben's work never smells of the swipe file. He looked at the best people, absorbed what they had to teach him, and then went his own way.

In this album we can watch the Corben style as it develops and matures. From the beginning, his sense of color was exquisite and original. Some of the earlier pictures are, for my taste, over-detailed, a hair too tight; he had to learn what every artist eventually learns: when to finish. For me, Corben is at his mature and confident best when he is most loose. That is when he is also his most fearless; he goes to a page knowing that the page cannot defeat him, that work will come off

that page, when he is through, that has never before existed in the world. Again, like the great artists and the most brilliant musicians.

With some artists, you wish you could function as a fight manager and show the artist how to use his strengths and minimize his weaknesses. You don't feel that way with the mature work of Richard Corben. Somehow, during the long years when he was working as a commercial draftsman at an industrial conglomerate called Calvin Communications, Inc., Corben became his own manager. He tried various idioms, mastered them, discarded them, and what remained was Richard Corben.

And being Richard Corben is no small thing. He is in his mature years now, and you don't ever wish for him to embark on specific projects. You wait, and you look. He will always do one thing: he will surprise us. We can ask nothing more of an American artist than that.

GALLERY

STATS

Name: Daniel Torres
Born: 1958
Bred: Valencia, Spain
Medium: Gouache
Hobby: The Cinema

GALLERY

STATS:
Name: Dovilio Brero
Born: February 14, 1950
Current Residence: Monasterolo, Italy

The Moon

Exit from Eden

Betrayal

Bionic Ark

Fashion's Demise

Robot's Hell

Gallery

PETER KUPER

STATS:
BORN: September 22, 1958
BRED: Cleveland, Ohio. Currently resides in New York City.
MEDIUM: "Whatever I get my hands on."
HOBBIES: Traveling.

"A lot of people look at my work and say it is a scary, dark, depressing, fearful, angst-ridden, paranoid view of the underbelly of society.... These people are correct."

"Of course, in an age of madness, to expect to be untouched by madness is a form of madness."
—Saul Bellow

"**I** can't work in only one style or medium too long without getting bored. I find that style is like clothing— if I wear it too long it starts to stink."

GALLERY

LES EDWARDS

I was born in 1949—in September, which for astrologers makes me a Virgo. Virgos are neat, organized, and tidy—so much for astrology. For the first year of my life I lived in Walthamstow, East London. I was a noisy baby, I cried a lot—so much for Walthamstow.

From there to East Ham, also in East London, where I lived until I went to art school in 1968. The local schools did their best with me. All I can remember of junior school is being ill quite a lot, and the school plays, though what I was doing in school plays I cannot imagine, since nowadays nothing would entice me into any kind of public performance. I did put aside my dramatic career long enough to pass the Eleven Plus exam, which provided my passport to nearby East Ham Grammar School for Boys. At this quite ludicrous place short trousers and caps were compulsory in the first year, despite the fact that some twelve-year-olds were nearly six feet tall.

Apart from art, my main interests were English literature and physics. Unfortunately the school's system did not permit the study of these three subjects to "A" level. One had to choose either "Arts" or "Sciences," carefully preventing the acquisition of a truly balanced education. Although I was forced to drop physics I have maintained an interest in the subject, and one of my more futile pastimes is trying to get my brain around quantum theory. As this is

Excerpted from *Blood & Iron* © GW Books and Les Edwards.

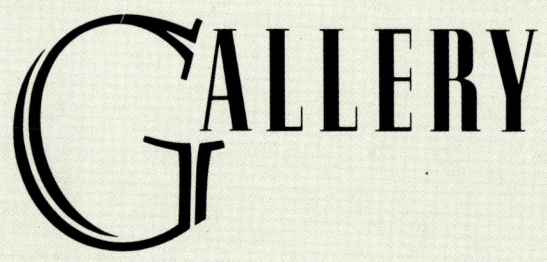

Alien Landscapes

The Priestess

The Ghoul

Conan the Rebel

Aztec

only really explicable in terms of advanced mathematics, of which I have absolutely no knowledge, this provides hours of harmless amusement. I'm quite convinced that they just make it up as they go along.

I had a fairly bright academic career, plenty of exams passed, etc., but once in the sixth form, I spent most of my time either in the Art Room, or pondering what I'd do when I got there. The two Art teachers—Dave Waterhouse and Wayne Stephenson—were encouraging, supportive, and constructively critical, all the things that teachers are supposed to be and so often aren't. It was under their influence that I applied to Hornsey College of Art.

1968 was the year of the famous student riots in Paris and the less famous "sit-in" at Hornsey. When I arrived there in November—the term was late starting because of the "trouble"—the college was in a state of confusion, and, fairly quickly, so was I. However, if it was confusing, it was also exciting and new to me. Too much has been written about the late sixties already for me to be able to add anything new, except perhaps to mention that the epithet "aging hippie" is often hurled in my direction. One of my friends often refers to me as that "Commie-pinko-poofter-artist," so you can see the sort of people I hang around with.

After the one year Foundation course, I went on to the Graphic Design course, which also offered illustration. The supposed "quality" of this course is one of my favorite hobby-horses, but I won't indulge it here. Suffice it to say that at the end of the three years I had very little more idea about illustration than I had at the start; my work and my confidence both suffered.

In 1973, at the end of the course Diploma Show, a character called John Spencer turned up; at the time he was running a small illustrators' agency, Young Artists, from his home. He sought me out in a nearby pub with an offer to represent me and two of the other students. I cannot imagine what he saw in my work, which was of nothing like a professional standard, but it was agreed that if I could provide some samples of sufficient quality he would try to get me work. It took me a long time to bring my work up to an

untitled

acceptable level, but John was always both encouraging and critical, and in time work began to come my way. John left YA some time ago, and is now being a rock 'n' roll star, among other things. When John left, YA was taken over by Alison Eldred, who quickly became the world's best agent. Her endless enthusiasm and energy are astonishing.

In 1978 I moved from Hornsey back to the East End of London. I now live in Ilford with Valerie, a Director and Partner in Young Artists, without whom all this would be pointless, and two Siberian Huskies—Myska and Zera, without whom life would be considerably less hectic, but also less fun.
—**Les Edwards**

GALLERY

Ecstasy

JULIE BELL

As a bodybuilder my body is my medium. I sculpt and shape each muscle with a combination of power, control, and sensitivity. I have to recognize the need for balance—one body part can not overwhelm the others with strength or size. If this happens, the whole body is thrown off balance. Injury could occur and the aesthetics of the body diminish. Bodybuilding has taught me not only discipline, but that I am capable of pushing way beyond what I had ever dreamed possible.

I approach my painting the same way. I need a balanced composition, precise control in rendering, love and attention to each detail, sensitivity to color, warmth, and movement—and it all has to relate to itself. The fantasy art I am attracted to is centered around the figure and my love for the human body pushes me in that direction. I let myself be led by my paintings as I am working on them. Rigidity can kill a painting—spontaneity allows it to take on a life of its own.

As a woman, fantasy art is very appealing to me. I love the romance of it—the lusty, sexual side of it as well as the fairy tale side. I love the sensuality that comes from strength and power in men and women. My two children have always been a great source of inspiration and life's lessons for me. Watching them discover their own strengths is an emotional experience for me. I have always been an intensely romantic person and now I have my opportunity to share it with the world. That's extremely fulfilling for a romantic exhibitionist like myself.

—*Julie Bell*

Serpent Sage

I am a bodybuilder. I am an artist.
I am a woman.

Battle of the Mer

Young Wizard

To Become a Man

Untitled

Peter Kuper's COMICS TRIPS

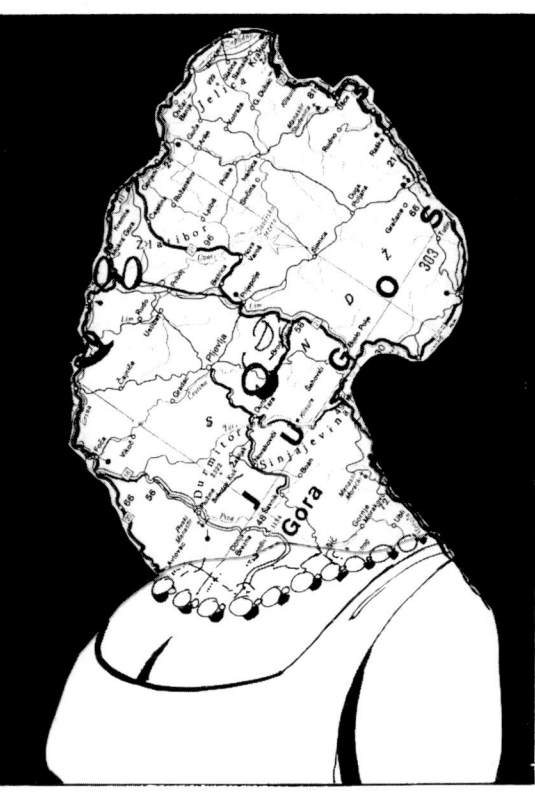

TRAVELLERS I HATED
- Germans: loud, self-centered, egotists
- French: snobby, self-centered, egotists
- Israelis: rude, egotists
- Australians: loud, obnoxious, mannerless
- some English: stuff-shirt, boring, rude
- Californians: brainless, inane, obnoxious
- most other Americans: whiny, loud, overt tourists

TRAVELLERS I LIKED
- Dutch: attractive, bright, relaxed
- Swedanish: same as above minus bright
- Austrians: intelligent, friendly, although some Master Race attitude holdover
- some English: witty, friendly, semi-informed
- New Zealanders: good travellers, fun, relaxed
- French: how can you hate people who love comix?!

"Of course, it wasn't by accident that my wife, Betty and I found ourselves globe-trotting through Africa and Southeast Asia. We had been fantasizing about and saving for this trip for years."

COPYRIGHT © 1992 PETER KUPER. ALL RIGHTS RESERVED.
PUBLISHED BY TUNDRA PUBLISHING, LTD.

"This was travel

with a capital "T"—Indiana Jones, Lawrence of Arabia, The Year of Living Dangerously, The African Queen, The Man Who Would be King! Vacations are for tourists anxious to disengage, relax and watch their time evaporate. What we were looking for was high-adventure. Unexplored regions, 18-hour bus rides, bizarre infections: we wanted to throttle the experiences for all they were worth— and then lie on the beach for a week."

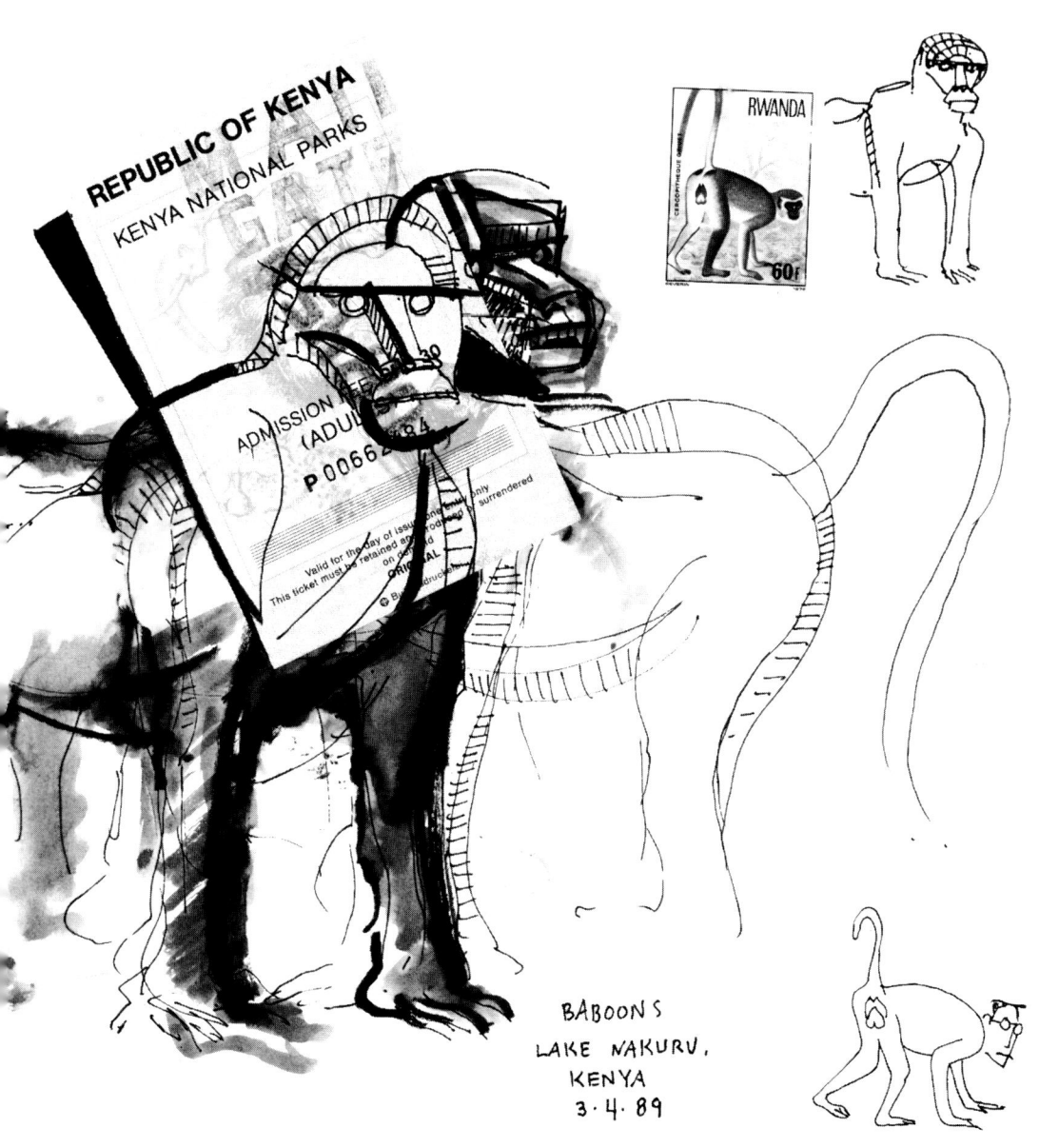

BABOONS
LAKE NAKURU,
KENYA
3·4·89

"When wrestling

with some nasty microbe or another, one has ample opportunity to squat or double over and reflect on one's life. I found this problem could be avoided with a few simple steps:

1. Develop new annoying habits.
2. Consume a magic mushroom omelette.
3. Scuba dive without training.
4. Rent a motorcycle (helmets not included).
5. Don't go on the trip expecting to become Lawrence of Arabia.

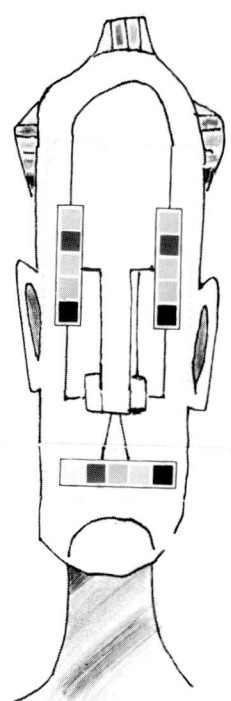

The process of communicating these designs to a Balinese mask maker was probably the deepest conversation I've had without words. Through drawing, gesturing, and laughing, I commissioned him to carve (counter-clockwise) Just-New-In-Town-Take-My-Money, Constipation, and Lost/Stolen Passport masks.

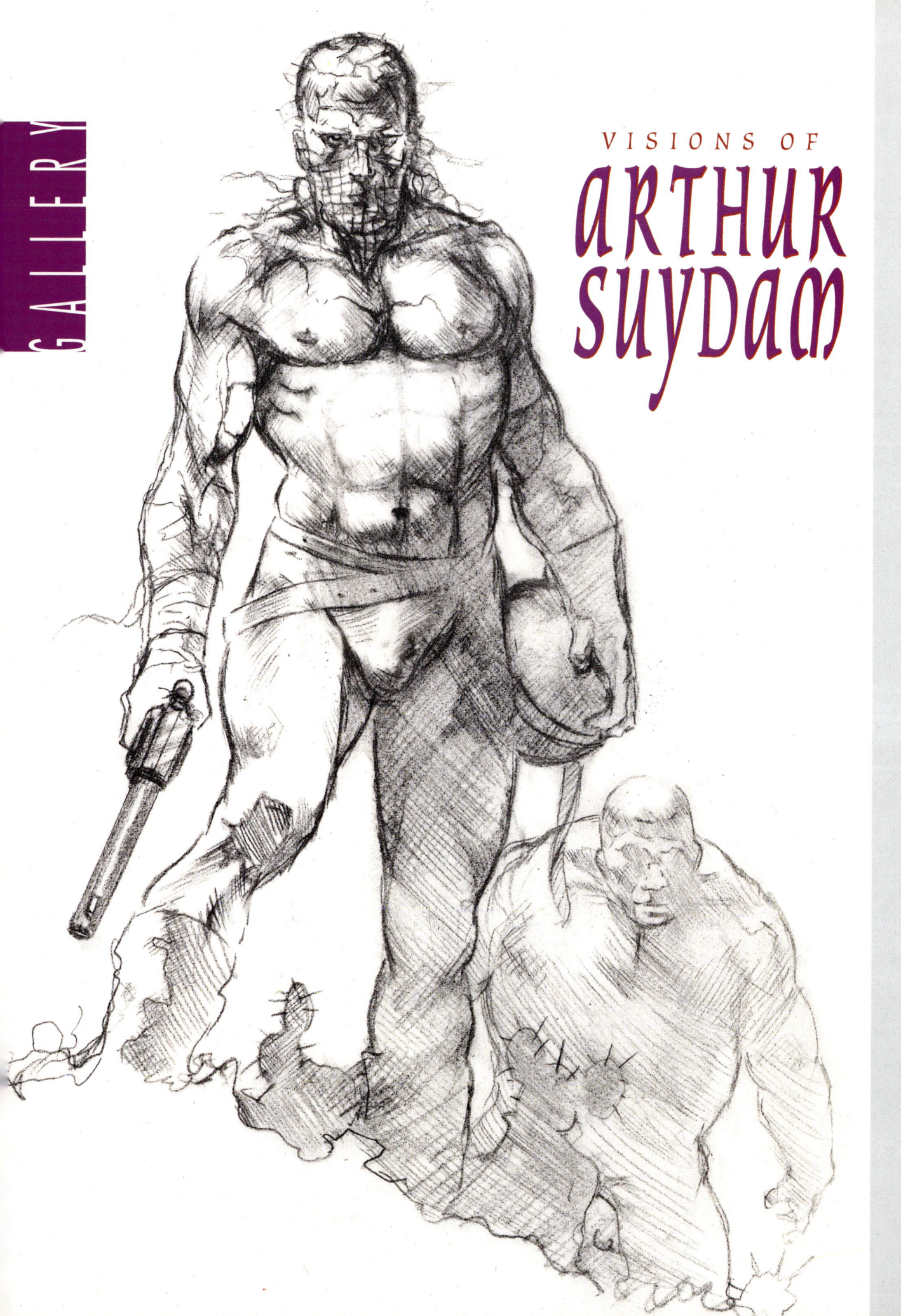

ARTHUR SUYDAM

grew up in New Jersey where he began drawing at the age of four. While in high school, he found his uncle's Famous Artists Course workbooks, where he discovered the illustrations of his major influences; Albert Dorne and Norman Rockwell. Early on, Suydam came across EC Comics and devoured the work of Graham "Ghastly" Ingels. When the early *Creepy* magazines began to appear, he once again found horror to his liking and would be forever inspired by Frank Frazetta. Arthur's very first published work appeared in *Creepy* on the fan letters page.

In 1973, Suydam began illustrating horror scripts for DC Comics' *House of Secrets*. His submissions were deemed "too adult" for the young audience of mainstream comics. He found a home at *Heavy Metal*

Magazine. There he developed "Mudwogs" which later continued at Continuity Comics. A fully painted, intensely-detailed "Mudwogs" graphic novel is due for release in 1995.

Much of Suydam's art reflects a fascination for things reptilian. "I've spent a lot of time in the South, in Florida, exploring swamps, catching snakes… even catching alligators with a rope. The textures of reptile skin fascinate me. I had my own alligator for thirteen years. It only grew to four feet, though. Maybe life in Trenton, New Jersey, didn't agree with it."

Just published from Dark Horse Comics is *Visions: The Art of Arthur Suydam*, which he says "reflects my best work to date". A deluxe limited-edition of the book will be created exclusively for the Alexander Gallery of New York City, where an exhibit of the original art will be shown.

GALLERY

Simon Bisley is Britain's most famous export of recent years. His stylized renderings of big guns and over-exaggerated muscles have taken the world's comic market by storm. Looking like one of his characters (six feet tall with required leather jacket), Simon's main loves are cars and motorcycles.

Influenced by the work of Richard Corben and Frank Frazetta, Simon Bisley practiced his illustration techniques during a stint at art college. His powerful images of ultra-dramatic ultra violence were looked upon there as a waste of time. Moving to London, this grim, engine-grease loving, Heavy Metal fan found jobs doing album cover art which garnered appearances in *Rock Power*. The first time he ever tried a sequential strip was for *2000 A.D.* with the *A.B.C. Warriors* and it just took off. This led to work on the daily newspaper strip *Judge Dredd*. Bisley's no-nonsense attitude made this futuristic Dirty Harry character an instant smash in Great Britain.

Judgment On Gotham, a Judge Dredd crossover with America's popular caped crime fighter Batman, brought Simon Bisley's talent into the spotlight here in the U.S. as well. Capable of creating with great speed (producing six or more finished pages a day) he has amassed an impressive portfolio in just a few years. His work on *Doom Patrol*, *Grendel*, *Judge Dredd*, *Lobo*, *Melting Pot*, *Slaine*, and *Swamp Thing* have guaranteed them best sellers. He is currently collaborating with his *Melting Pot* partners Kevin Eastman and Eric Talbot on a top secret new project due later this year.

WHILE VISITING HIS OLD BUDDY AND *MELTING POT* CO-CREATOR, KEVIN EASTMAN, SIMON BISLEY DISCOVERED THE MOVIE MAGIC OF DIRECTOR JOHN WOO. AFTER VIEWING THE BLOODY CLASSICS *THE KILLER*, *HARDBOILED*, AND *BULLET IN THE HEAD*, SIMON WAS HOOKED AND INCORPORATED MR. WOO'S INFLUENCE INTO THEIR NEW COMIC *BODYCOUNT*.

IT'S THE CLASSIC TALE OF HIT MEN, HIT WOMEN, CONTRACTS, BETRAYAL, WORLDWIDE MOB DISPUTES, PAWNS, KINGPINS, BABES, BULLETS, DYNAMITE, DETECTIVES, FBI, AN EX-HOCKEY PLAYER, AND A TURTLE.

THIS FOUR ISSUE COLOR SERIES IS BEING PUT OUT BY THOSE TALENTED THUGS AT IMAGE COMICS AND WILL HIT STORES IN MARCH 1996.

BODYCOUNT IS JUST THE START OF THE TURTLE/IMAGE COLLABORATION. ERIK LARSON, CREATOR OF THE BEST-SELLING SAVAGE DRAGON COMIC SERIES, WILL KICK OFF A WHOLE NEW SERIES OF MUTANT NINJA TURTLES IN JULY. FOR INFO, CONTACT MIRAGE STUDIOS AT (413)586-7066.

GALLERY

Gil Bruvel

MIDNIGHT

THE REALITY OF A DREAMER

Gil Bruvel knew from early on that his destiny was to be an artist. After moving from Sydney, Australia to the town of Istres in the south of France, Gil devoted most of his time to his artistic abilities. He was so engrossed in his art that he left his studies at a private boarding school in order to pursue what would become his life's work. Bruvel got much of his inspiration from master restorer Laurent De Montcassin of the Louvre's Master Restoration Workshop whom he spent many intense years studying under. It was not until his late teens that Gil made it on his own. At sixteen years of age, the gifted artist displayed his "visionary" style paintings at the Musee de Baux-de-Provence, in Baux-de-Provence, France. The show got rave reviews.

Bruvel likes for his work to be considered "visionary", since his inspiration comes from a state of mind rather than being thought of as "surrealistic". According to Gil, surrealism is based solely on dreams and he feels his ability to "dream up" the images he uses in his paintings is solely a result of using his conscious imagination. This style of art has made him an enormous success worldwide. His art has been displayed in the United States, Japan, and many European nations. Bruvel is one of the youngest recipients of the notable Palais des Congres award, given by the Minister of Culture of France.

BALANCED UPON THE TIP OF THE FINGER

MEMORY

INFINITESIMAL CITY

THE NIGHT

THE HALLUCINATED CITY

In Gil's work, you can often recognize the familiar. However, because of his visionary style, Gil often transforms ordinary things, such as fruit and wine glasses into new concepts with their own space and volume, changing them into something greater. Bruvel believes it is important to see beyond the obvious, to realize that things are not always what they appear to be. Through his work, you may possibly recognize something from nature such as a shell that has been transformed into a gate. Bruvel often enjoys leaving the reality of his visions to the viewer, to discover...

THE REALITY OF A DREAMER.

You can now purchase some of Gil Bruvel's work. Turn to page 24 for ordering details.

AWAKENING

GALLERY

BY TAYYAR OZKAN
Reachable at http://www.concentric.net/~tayyar

TAYYAR OZKAN WAS BORN IN TURKEY IN 1962. AT 16, HE PUBLISHED HIS FIRST CARTOON IN A LOCAL POLITICAL NEWSPAPER. OVER THE NEXT FEW YEARS, TAYYAR'S WORK WAS PUBLISHED IN SEVERAL HUMOR MAGAZINES AND NEWSPAPERS. HE ALSO ILLUSTRATED CHILDREN'S BOOKS AND GREETING CARDS.

IN 1989 TAYYAR MOVED TO THE UNITED STATES. UPON HIS ARRIVAL, HE WORKED MOSTLY ON GRAPHIC AND TEXTILE DESIGN. THEN, IN 1992 *WORLD WAR 3 ILLUSTRATED* WAS PUBLISHED. SINCE THEN, THE WORK HASN'T STOPPED.

TAYYAR'S *CAVE MAN* CREATION APPEARED IN HEAVY METAL IN 1993. IN 1994, HE COLLABORATED WITH WRITER JOEL ROSE AND AMOS POE TO PRODUCE THE MYSTERY BOOK, *La PACIFICA* FOR PARADOX/DC COMICS. TAYYAR'S BOOKS, *BUSHWHACKED, CAVE BANG*, AND *PET* HAVE BEEN PUBLISHED IN EROS COMIX. HE HAS ASO INKED THE DREAMING FOR VERTIGO/DC.

TODAY, TAYYAR LIVES IN HIS FAVORITE CITY -- NEW YORK. HE SPENDS MOST OF HIS TIME WORKING ON THE CAVE MAN SERIES.

HAVE WE REALLY EVOLVED? THIS COLLECTION OF SILENT GAG STRIPS PRESENTS MANY A SITUATION STARTING WITH CAVEMEN AND ENDING WITH OURSELVES IN OUR SUPPOSED MODERN TIMES. WE BUILT MEGALOPOLISES AND FANCY TECHNOLOGIES BUT, AS OZKAN SHOWS US WITH A SLY GRIN, DEEP INSIDE, WE'RE STILL JUST A BUNCH O' GRUNTING BEASTS!

GALLERY

ROB ATTENDED THE UNIVERSITY OF TOLEDO, THE ART INSTITUTE OF PITTSBURGH AND CARNEGIE MELON. ROB HAS WORKED FOR SUCH CLIENTS AS TWENTIETH CENTURY FOX, LUCAS FILMS, PARAMOUNT PICTURES, MARVEL COMICS, TODD McFARLANE PRODUCTIONS, AND MANY OTHERS. HE ALSO HAS JUST FINISHED 2 JULIE STRAIN POSTERS AND ONE LITHOGRAPH.

ROB'S LATEST PROJECT IS A BOOK CALLED "LOST HEROES", A FULLY PAINTED PHOTO REALISTIC COMIC, BOTH WRITTEN AND PAINTED BY ROB. THE BOOK STARS MARK HAMILL, JASON CARTER, PAT TALLMAN, WALTER KOENIG, RICHARD BIGGS, PETER JURASIC, JEFF WILERTH, DENNY SCHAFER, JULIE STRAIN, KEVIN EASTMAN, TODD McFARLANE, ROBIN DOWNS AND MANY OTHERS.

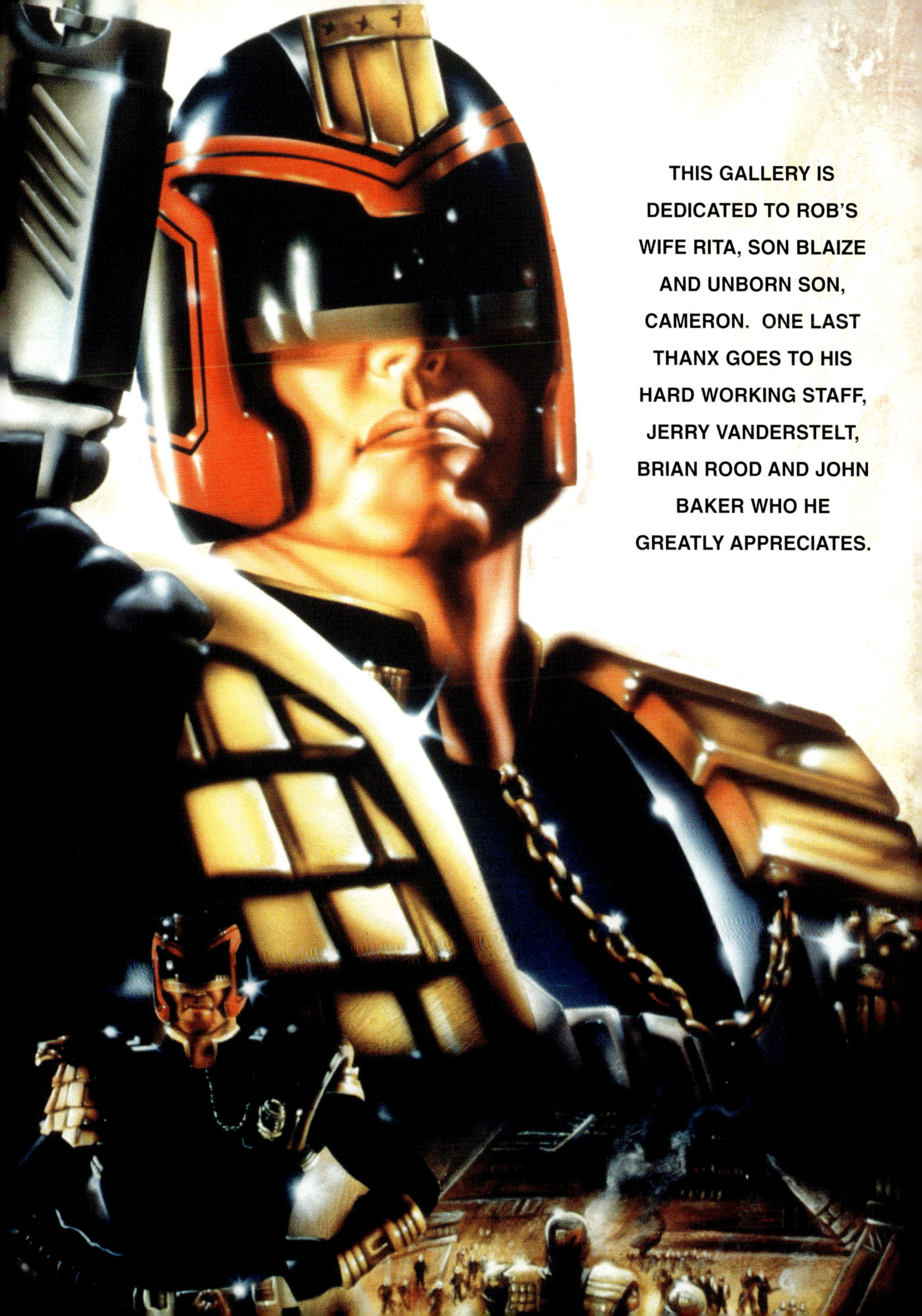

THIS GALLERY IS DEDICATED TO ROB'S WIFE RITA, SON BLAIZE AND UNBORN SON, CAMERON. ONE LAST THANX GOES TO HIS HARD WORKING STAFF, JERRY VANDERSTELT, BRIAN ROOD AND JOHN BAKER WHO HE GREATLY APPRECIATES.

Dorian's years as a commercial illustrator left him unfulfilled and with a compelling desire to accomplish more in the area that would enable him to give full vent to his talents and creativity. Fantasy art has become the means that has allowed him to step into areas where imagination combined with the female form permit limitless regions for his brush to explore.

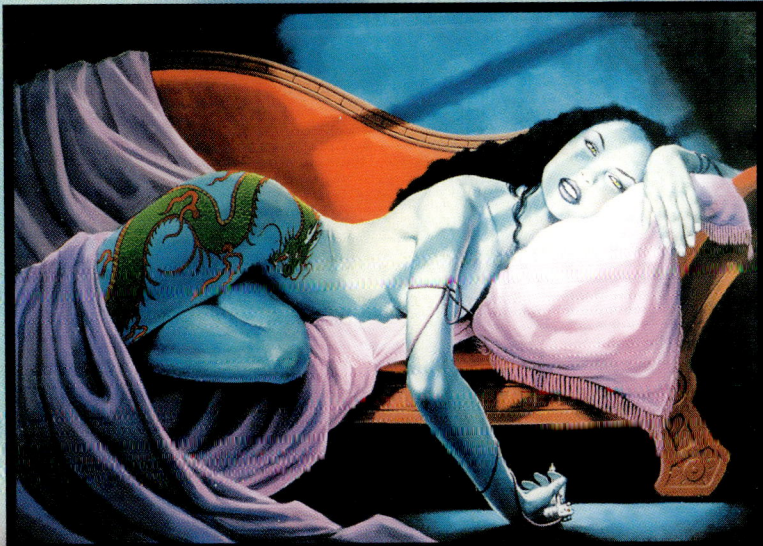

His studio in Pittsburgh is filled with paintings and drawings that have been done over the years in all media, from pencil through oils on canvas. He has settled primarily on painting with acrylics on illustration board, achieving results with this generally considered difficult medium that astounded many of his peers in the art field. He prefers acrylics as a means to achieve the appearance of oils yet allowing a production time of two to three days per painting because of its fast drying characteristics.

Although a relative newcomer to the fantasy industry, Dorian's work can be seen on numerous comic book covers, card sets and in art galleries around the world.

For more info on upcoming products by Dorian, write to:
SSP C/O Dorian
P.O. Box 51172
Philadelphia, Pa. 19115

BLUE AMBER

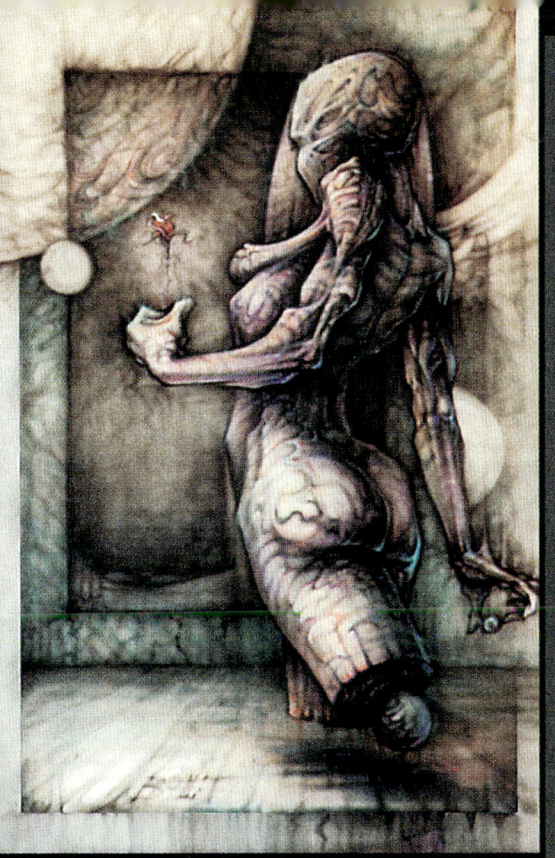

WAITING AT THE WINDOW
(LOVE IN ONE HAND, HOPE IN THE OTHER)

As a child I was the victim of a profound and frightening imagination. By drawing pictures of the demons and monsters that plagued me I could gain some sense of understanding"

LAS VEGAS BUTTERFLY GIRL
I COULD DETECT THE LIGHT FRAGRANCE OF FLOWERS THROUGH THE THICK SMELL OF BLOOD."

SHADES OF AMBER

SCARECROW

KINETIC MEMORY

JENNIFER

The art of David Bollt illuminates a vast and complex symbol language for the viewer. A language that describes a temple, ancient and mysterious, ranging from the darkest and most disturbing of places to the brightest and most spiritual of mountain tops. His art paints a picture of the soul, balanced by dark and light in all its changing and eternal forms. Many of these timeless images touch a place in us all as they rise from the mists of our own preconscious memories.

David Bollt was born on February 6, 1971, in Far Rockaway, NY. He grew up in south Florida where he studied fine art and illustration at the Ringling School of Art and Design. David went back to New York to study the ancient art of tattooing, and has been working as a professional tattoo artist since 1993. He now lives and works in Pompano Beach, Fl.

Visit the
Mind's Eye Gallery
at http://www.artspace.com
to enter the lush and frightening
imagination of David Bollt.

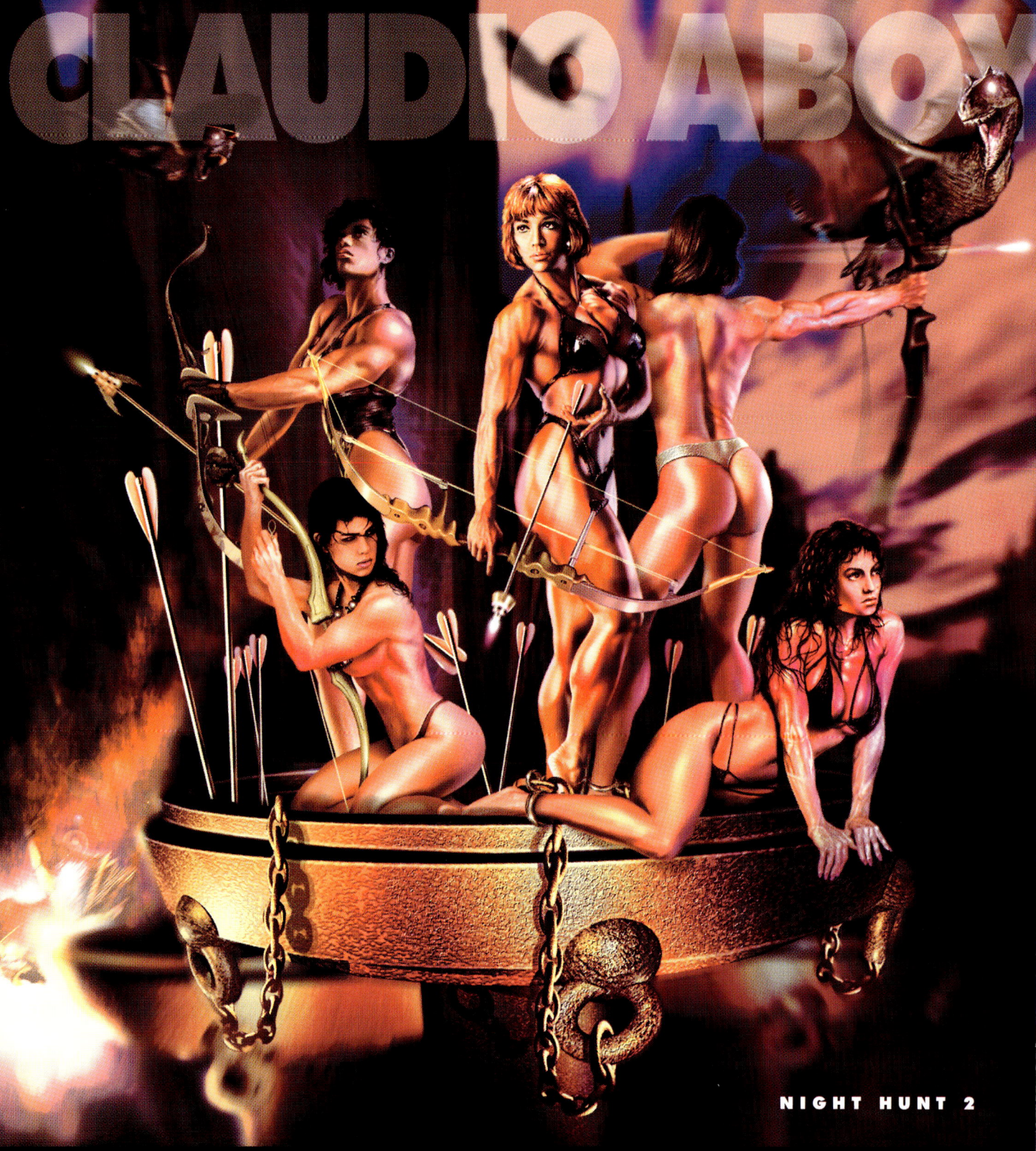

NIGHT HUNT 2

G A L L E R Y

Claudio Aboy was born in Argentina on January 24th 1959. At a young age he began his study of drawing at several different art schools. Being a comic fan, Aboy decided to pursue comic drawing. Self taught in advertising illustration techniques, especially in airbrushing, he made this field his means of life. At the same time, Claudio produced fantasy illustrations as a hobby. Later this hobby became his main area of work.

NIGHT HUNT

SENTRY

In 1994, Aboy began working with digital illustration. Today, he uses digital techniques to retouch mixed media illustrations as well as fully digital hyperrealistic illustrations. His digital illustrations are completely original; he does not scan any part of them. Among traditional techniques, his favorites are oil and color pencil.

PILOT 3

SOLDIER 1

PILOT 1

SWORD IN THE STONE

DEFENSELESS

Claudio's artwork has appeared on comic book covers, posters and record covers throughout Latin America and Europe. He has participated in many exhibitions and shows such as those organized by the Society of Illustrators of New York, of which he has been a member of for several years.

GALLERY
John Zeleznik

◆ TALIZ ◆

◆ An independent illustrator since 1987, John graduated from the Otis/Parsons Institute of Art in Los Angeles with a BFA in Illustration. Role playing game covers have been a major part of his career since 1989. His clients have included Mattel Toys, Berkeley Books, The Fasa Corporation, Steve Jackson Games, and Palladium Books.

◆ HARDWEAR ◆

◆ LEAN 3 ◆

◆ SUMMER ON VALONE ◆

◆ DUO ◆

◆ He works on illustration board with acrylic paints and has recently entered the digital medium using Photoshop.

◆ John has had works in the Society of Illustrators: West show as well as the "Pavilion of Wonder" science fiction/fantasy show at the Canton Museum of Art.

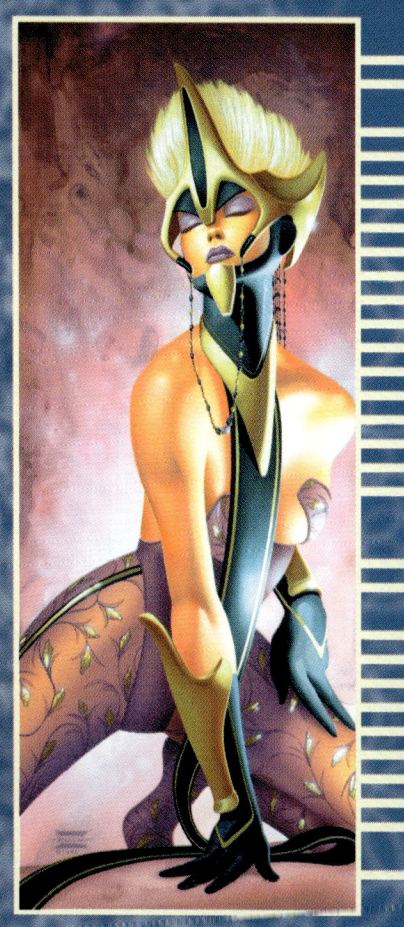

◆ DIZDEM ◆

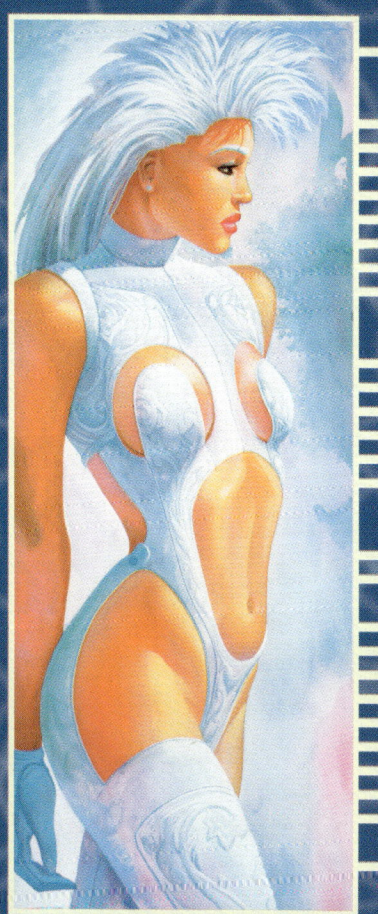

◆ WINTER MAIDEN ◆

◆ For the past five years his works have been featured in the art book SPECTRUM: The Best in Contemporary Fantastic Art.

◆ SEETHING DIVINITY ◆

◆ Recently John has released his own line of limited prints, posters, portfolios and t-shirts featuring his work.

◆ RAZE ◆

PROHIBITED book

LUIS ROYO

HEAVY METAL

LUIS ROYO
A **PROHIBITED** INTERVIEW

Having published five art-books (**Women, Malefic, Secrets, III Millennium** and **Dreams**), **Luis Royo** ranks among the most relevant illustrators in the world. The mix of his quick pencils and the accurate use of the airbrush has created the most beautiful women, the most exciting worlds and the most surprising creatures.

No genre or technique escapes his mastery, and it's been his constant restlesness that has driven him to produce **Prohibited Book**, his new and most surprising work, whose main protagonist is sexual desire.

Prohibited Book is Royo's first work conceived as a book from beginning to end. All the illustrations, more than thirty, have been created exclusively for this publication, so they have never been seen before. It is also remarkable that **Prohibited Book** has been conceived from the beginning as a trilogy, so a new book will appear in the two next years. Another interesting feature is that the artist's son, **Rómulo**, has collaborated actively, both with several pictures, also of sexual character, and in the book's graphic design.

There's no doubt that **Prohibited Book** is a breath of originality and fresh air in the world of illustration, and its publication will arouse many comments (all of them positive, we're sure). Before everyone forms an opinion, we have let the artist speak about his interesting proposal.

PROHIBITED BOOK means a new turn in your career. What were you looking for, what did you want to communicate?

In every book, I look for a new road, with new approaches. The previous one, **DREAMS**, was a collection of works of every genre and style, it was mostly a challenge towards my capacity to face the different genres, each one with its keys, its tonalities, its message...
PROHIBITED BOOK is just the contrary. I want the reader to dive into the world of eroticism, going down to the bottom, and I try to look at it directly, stripping it of color, puritanism... everything. Whereas in all of my previous works, each image is a small story, in this case I only wanted to represent just an image, sex and its pure message, without any embellishment. My intention was to undress even my own dreams, to share them face to face with the reader, both nude, with our darkest thoughts and desires on the table.

Your audience should not be surprised with this change, since you have always innovated somehow with each new book.

It's true. In all the books I have tried to change something in relation to the previous one, and I have always waited for the results totally panicked. The first one, **WOMEN**, is a book with bright colors and clean lights; the beauty and femininity I tried to represent is athletic, healthy, heroic. When I was preparing the following one, **MALEFIC**, I left behind everything from **WOMEN**, studied the Tenebrist movement and changed to chiaroscuro, to darker images, enjoying myself in a fantastic-medieval age. In **SECRETS** I took refuge in the mists, in a canon of beauty much younger and softer, contrasting with the Beast and the threatening landscape. When I had nearly forgotten science-fiction, the genre where I made my name in the first place, I started **III MILLENNIUM**. I removed many colors from the palette, recalling the theme of the catastrophic obsession that seizes mankind at each end of a millennium, I retook sci-fi from a different view, merging it with elements from our society such as advertisements, holidays, cars, etc., looking for plastic clashes in the pictures.

> My intention was to undress even my own dreams, to share them face to face with the reader.

Why this obsession with changes?

I always try to find a new challenge when I look at the blank surface of paper. I think it is very important to feel the doubt, to feel the emptiness in your belly; that makes you feel good with your job. It is essential not to fall into routine, so that what you do is always alive, and I'm sure the reader perceives this.

Another surprising aspect of Prohibited Book is the fact that you have planned it as a trilogy.

Yes, it was the only way I could express all that I felt. In this first book I've tried to represent a never-ending range of brown tones, looking for a pure eroticism. I think that the second one will be full of cold colors, bluish and greenish greys, to merge sex and metals (cold lights, pale skins and machines), a sex born out of cold, which is not the usual. The third book will be based on golden tones, both in sex and atmosphere, playing with the sfumatto, in order to live eroticism by the candlelight, as trying to recover lost desires. I really look forward to creating all these illustrations.

What do the terms "illustration" and "fantasy art" mean to you?

The old definition of "image serving the text" is no longer true. Nowadays, in many cases, image works on its own in the world of communication, and as such appears in many media; the message is the image itself. I think that what we call "fantasy art" has taken advantage of the new ways of industry and communication in order to survive, adapting itself to the most widespread media, such as book covers, magazines, computer games... and many others. It has looked for new readers, thus proving that it is alive.

Are we witnessing, then, a return to figurative art, where also the so-called "fantasy art" would be included?

Inside all this new "going back" to figurative art, there are many ways, some of them wrong. Lately, you can see again a still life, some hyperrealism from the sixties, and many other things that do not offer anything new. However, in what has been called "fantasy art" you can find again this typical creativity of mankind (and I would quote many authors included in this category). For me it is a terrain I feel very comfortable in, and it is the ideal place to dream, to let imagination fly.

Your working pace is incredibly fast. What makes you work with such intensity?

There are usually two steps. In the first one, the only thing that matters is what you are doing with yourself, it is like a private chat, a challenge towards yourself. I always try to have all my books include an intuitive part, so as they grow a continuous dialogue develops. Afterwards, there is another part in which the desire to communicate something takes the reins, and I want to find the reader, talk to him through my picture. I could summarize it as an attempt to share dreams through my works.

I'm sure you have several projects in mind...

Yes. I am very excited about the creation of a fantasy character which we will make introduce soon. I have studied the inner, psychological side of the character as well as the facade... I am very excited because, besides my illustrations, I want to be related to some character created by me. I also have some drawers full of material for a new book, searching in a very indefinite space and time, in which I want to represent a world impossible to conceive according to the laws of physics we know. To play with gravity, to change completely the appearance of the characters, to find a new way to represent beauty... in a rude word, to look for intangible things and desire them. But before, **PUFF OF DEVILS** will appear, a small booklet of pencilled drawings and comments about the Beauty-and-Beast theme that fascinates me so much, and which has always followed me throughout my career.

Days seem to get shorter...

Yes, very short indeed. I work almost fifteen hours a day, from Monday to Sunday, and even so I would like to stop the clocks, make them move slowly... though I think this is something that happens to many of us.

All the illustrations are © 1999 Luis Royo
Represented by NORMA Editorial

More information in
Luis Royo's official web page in
www.norma-ed.es/royo

Though the art I depict is dark, it does not mean I am a devil worshipper or a mentally disturbed psychic. I do what I do as a form of escape. I escape the bullshit of everyday rudeness and worries and enter my world- a playpen where inhibitions, imaginations, madness, fears and angers run wild in a frolicking orgy of psycho-bliss. In this world I am God, Passion is my disciple and Repression my Anti-Christ.

Contrary to what many believe, my childhood was actually quite normal. I was born the youngest child of three in the armpit of New York in 1969 under the sign of the Virgo. Life was quite normal until my college days at UC Berkeley where my experiences were should I say "mind altering". After attaining a Sociology degree at Cal., I decided to dedicate myself to art. I enrolled in San Jose State where I attained another Bachelors degree in Art History and a minor in Fine Arts.

Before I could contribute my art to the world, I had to know what was already out there. Today I work as a freelance designer / illustrator. My works have been featured in various publications including FX Art and Design, Juxtapox, Spectrum 5, Applied Arts and the upcoming Society of Illustrators Annual and Step By Step Illustration Annual.

See more on david's website: www.davidho.com

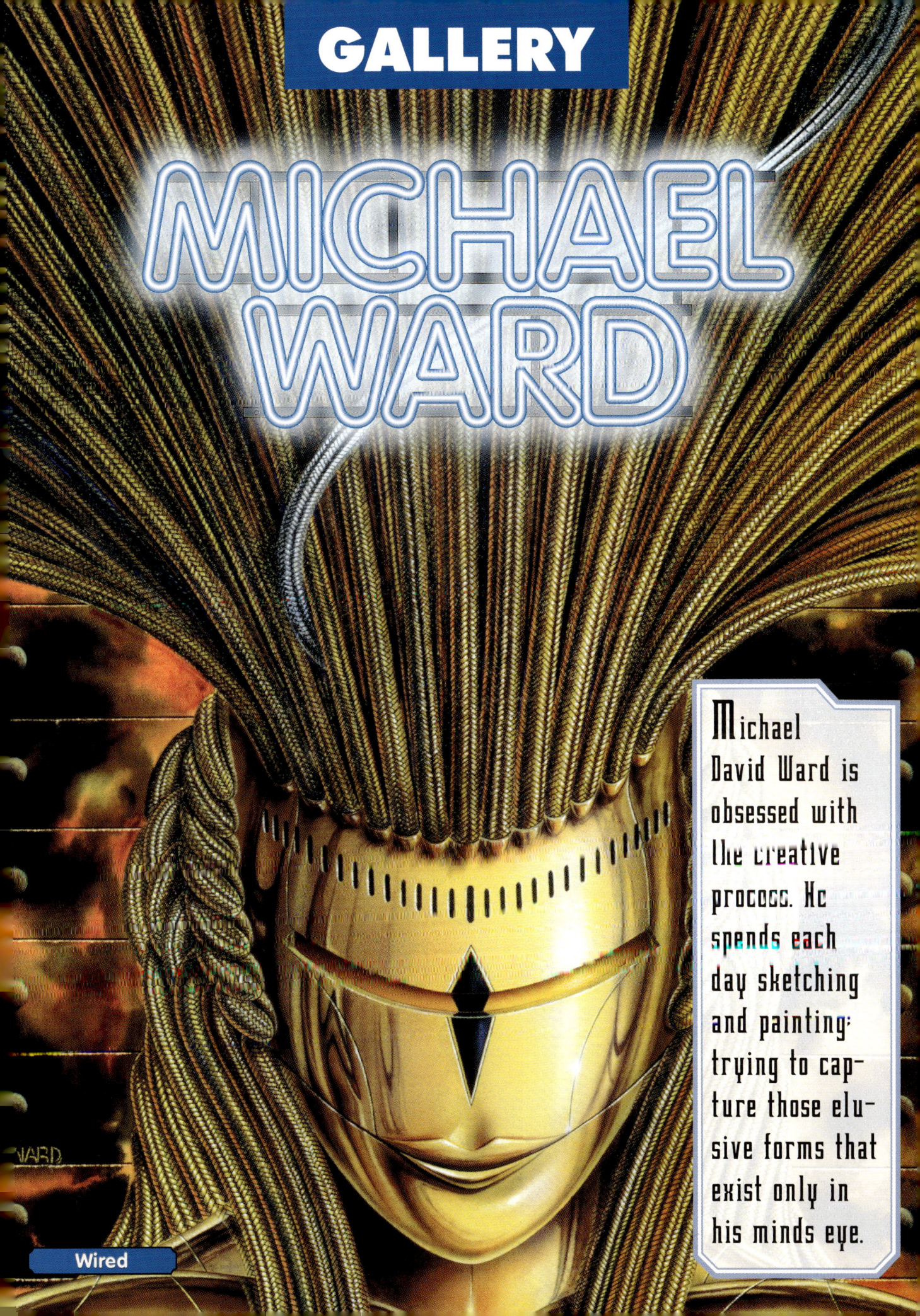

Ward has been exploring art since an early age and after pursuing a career in the high tech industry as a technical writer and illustrator, he finally made a full time commitment to freelancing and fine arts in 1987. During that time, while he sold many of his paintings in galleries across the country and internationally, Ward also started an action-sportswear company called Lifeforms, which featured his character designs.

After a number of years, the company became very successful, selling its clothing to stores all over the world. Ward finally sold his interest in the company to pursue more freely many of the ideas that personally excited him.

Automaton

Siren

Rising

The Oracle

Medusa

Nefertiti

Even Hollywood became interested in some of the character and story ideas that Ward created for his company which resulted in options by two major studios.

In between his own personal painting, Ward has created numerous commemorative works for Paramount Studios Star Trek, Lucas Art's Star Wars, and New Line Cinemas' Lost in Space. Many of the images he created have been licensed by companies and produced on products such as collector plates, prints, puzzles, calendars, trading cards, etc.

Mia

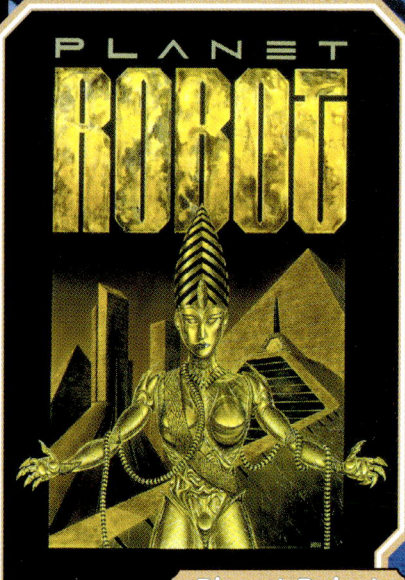
Planet Robot

Ward spends most of his time on his personal works where he can be completely free to pursue anything that comes to mind. Presently he is developing several science-fiction story projects, combining both his writing and paintings. Ward is excited at the prospect of exploring his characters through writing. He feels with story-telling, the characters can come to life.

Ward finds the imagination limitless in its ability to conjure up the fantastic and sees no end in sight for all the ideas that will provide him a lifetime's worth of visions to paint and write about.

Michael David Ward can be contacted by writing to:
Michael David Ward
P.O. Box 14396
Santa Rosa, CA 95402
E-Mail:
neomyth@aol.com

Speed Demon

Chrome Molly

GALLERY

JUSTICE HOWARD

PART ONE...THE INCEPTION...BY JUSTICE HOWARD

Let me hip you to the mechanics of how it all started.

It all commenced with a short trip to SWORD & STONE. It was at Jane's insistence that I ended up there. Tony Swatten is the owner of SWORD & STONE. I went to visit him with nothing else in mind than just to meet the man and see his wares. The collaboration was an act of God, born in and of itself. Jane kept saying, "You must see him...you'll go apeshit when you see his stuff!" She was absolutely right...especially about the "apeshit" part! As soon as I walked through the door, I completely lost my mind.

Headpiece from Marilyn Manson video

Blade by Little John

MODELS
In Jean of Arc armour: **JULIE STRAIN**
Blonde: **ELKE JENSEN** - 26 time Playboy Playmate
Brunette: **DEVIN DEVASQUEZ** - Playboy Playmate
Model on Rocks: **ARBAN**
Asian Model: **MIMI MIYAGI**
Page Four Model: **KIRA REED**

I was looking at the "blade" from the movie "BLADE," the Zorro sword, as well as the sword built for the CONAN the BARBARIAN tv series (The original sword for the CONAN movie was made by Jody Samson), the sword from HIGHLANDER 4, the Zorro movie sword, etc., etc., etc. (All were used later in this photo profile.

After the pile of drool had settled that I left on the floor directly under Tony's weapons...I mentioned to him that I was shooting JULIE STRAIN for a magazine cover that evening. Tony said he had worked with Julie on a few movies and he inquired as to what the styling of the shoot was to be. I told him that the magazine issue was called THE FEMININE MYSTIQUE.

So Tony walks over to a spot in his shop where this gorgeous chain mail piece was laying out and picks up another huge piece of armour. With his unique brand of blacksmith brilliance, Tony drops this bomb on his visiting fotog: "We'll why don't you shoot her like JOAN OF ARC? You can't get more feminist than that! Here, I'll lend you this armour and you can just bring it back tomorrow."

Well, tomorrow came and went, the shoot went flawlessly (well, of course it did. I was shooting JULIE STRAIN!!) and I ended up with some absolutely stunning images of Julie in Joan of Arc chain mail & armour. The sword we used in the Julie's shoot was, of course, her F.A.K.K. 2 sword from her movie. Julie is my favorite model (and friend) and I cherish the time I spend documenting her voluptuous from.

After the Julie shoot was completed and all her images had been processed, Julie suggested I continue on with the series and have the end result appear as a profile in HEAVY METAL.

Since they had never, ever featured a photographer before (Heavy Metal has always only published illustrators), I was jazzed to death by the factoring of this proposal.

So, I contacted Tony at SWORD & STONE once again and asked him if he'd like to initiate a collaboration for HEAVY METAL. Tony was up for it. I'm sure visions of naked femalian warrior princesses lounging around his shop might have sold him on the idea. So with that, I planned the shoot.

PART TWO...THE SHOOT

I had decided that the photo shoot would be story boarded and then broken down into three parts.

1. The Joan of Arc shoots with Julie were the first images and they were already "in the can." Those were taken against the black velvet backdrop right in the living room of Julie's own spacious residence.

Claw Sword

HIGHLANDER movie sword.

Head piece from Marilyn Manson video.

2. Would be photographed at Tony's shop, thereby giving it the "real-deal black-smith shop" feel, where we could shoot sparks behind the camera and the girls would wear all the swords and armour as props. For this shoot, I would use two Playboy Playmates, ELKE JEINSEN and DEVIN DEVASQUEZ. Elke is a blonde, Devin darkhaired. I wanted a sort of salt vs. pepper look. Light vs. dark. And no foam-domes!!!

3. This shoot would have more of a 1,000,000 Years B.C., "cave girl" kind of feel to it. So I decided to shoot it on some big rocks in Chatsworth, CA. It's the actual spot where they shoot all of the western movies. An outside shoot would give a different feel altogether to both indoor shoots I had already styled. I would use Arban (pronounced R-BONN) for this one. The knife that Arban used in the shoot was provided by LITTLE JOHN, a badass blademaker. That knife, with the birdface on the end of the handle and two skull-spawns by the blade, is now part of my private art collection. All of the other weapons, swords and costuming in the shoot, however, are from SWORD & STONE.

(Left) Elke with CONAN television series sword; (Right) Devin with Marines sword.

Marilyn Manson head piece with Soul Hunter scythe.

Blade by Little John.

Razor shoes & Soul Hunter scythe. The scythe was featured in the last season of *BABYLON 5*. The "Soul Hunters" were featured characters in this episode with Martin Sheen.

Well, that's about it, kiddies. That's how it came into play. I wanted to do a cross between Frazetta meets "Untamed Warrior Women." Or, Xena times 10. Without the collaboration of TONY SWATTEN this profile never would be have come to fruition. Also thanks to JANE McMANIGILL for the introduction which fused TONY and I together. Thanks to my gorgeous girls for being exciting canvases. The voluptuous palettes aiding me in my quest for beautiful imagery. Props to my pal Julie Strain for possessing the perameters from which all other models must be measured. And kudos to Tony Swatten, one rad, bad blacksmith.

Blade by Little John.

Check website www.justicehoward.com for more HEAVY METAL imagery.

GALLERY
Mike DeWeese

The Meat Tree 20"x29" Collage ©1999 Mike DeWeese

Eyes Open 12"x14" Collage ©1988 Mike DeWeese

Mike DeWeese creates unique imagery which combines elements of fantasy and fine art. The artist studied figure drawing and painting for four years at the Watts Atelier in San Diego, and he taught life drawing during his final year there. He likes to work with oils, charcoal, pen and ink, but his favorite medium is magazine collage. DeWeese's monster collage technique produces compelling images that are alien, yet strangely realistic. His dynamic compositions guide the viewers eye to the center of the action despite the rich detail of his subjects.

Mother Ship 18"x24" Oil ©1998 Mike DeWeese

Water Spout 12"x17" Collage ©1999 Mike DeWeese

Blind Date 12"x16" Collage with Acrylic ©1999 Mike DeWeese

Invasion of the Boyfriend Snatchers
10"x15" Pen & Ink ©1994 Mike DeWeese

Urge 16"x20" Oil ©1999 Mike DeWeese

Full Moon 24"x25" Pen & Ink ©1998 Mike DeWeese

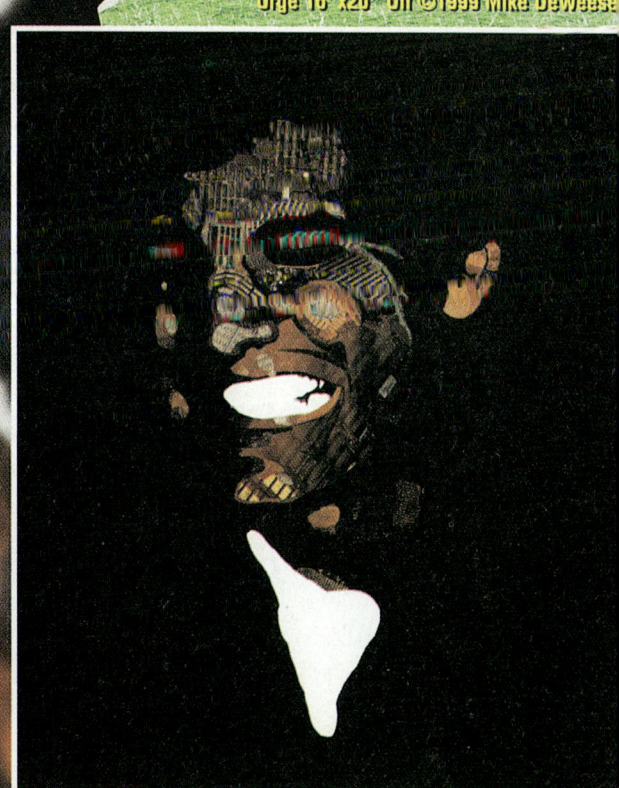

Grinner 15"x20" Collage ©1990 Mike DeWeese

Butterfly Avenger 19"x25" Collage ©2000 Mike DeWeese

Mike DeWeese's edgy collage work is unlike anything being done by other fantasy artists.

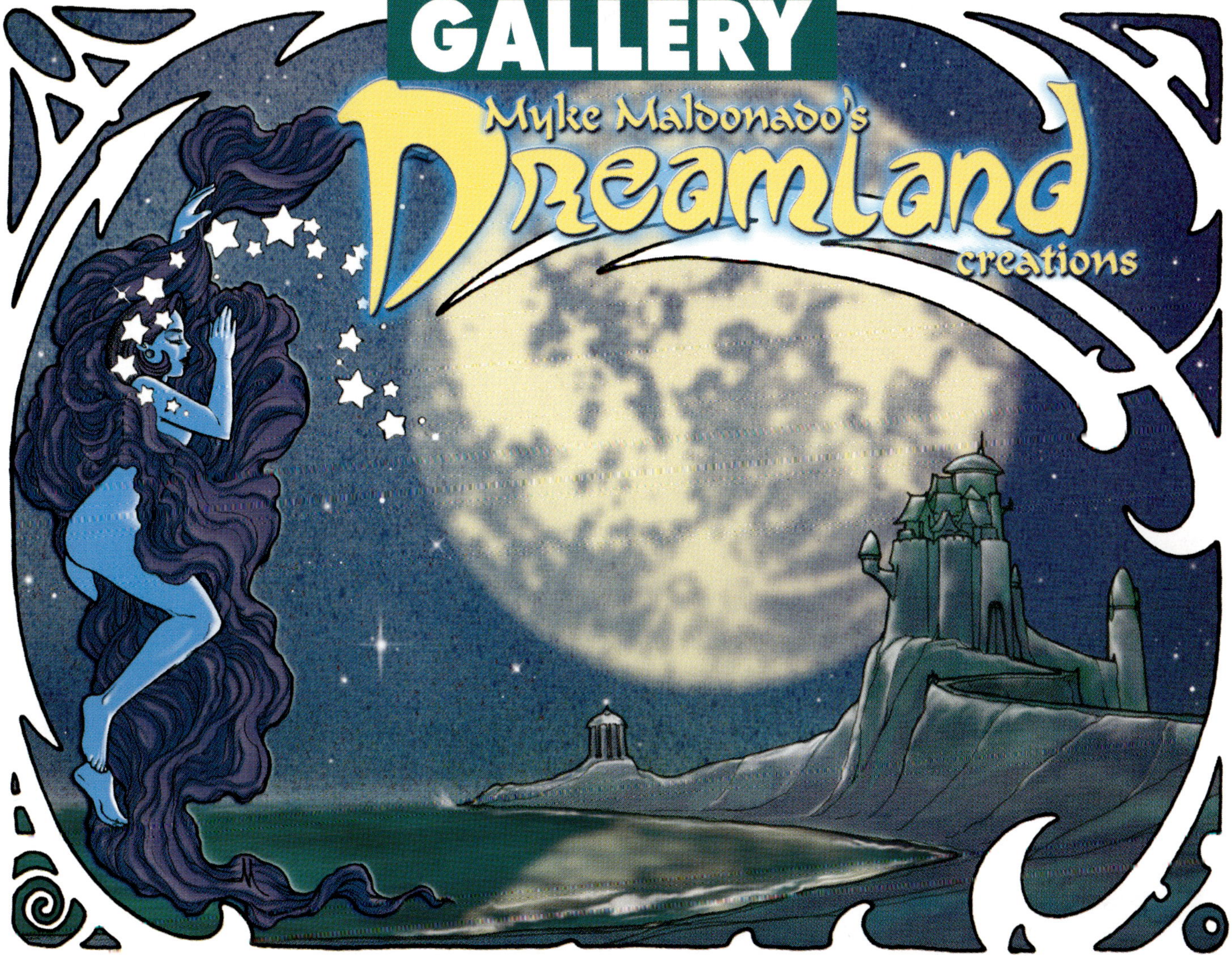

GALLERY
Myke Maldonado's Dreamland creations

"I've always been an artist. Since I can remember, it's always been something that's set me apart from other people."

Following my interest in art I attended the school of Art & Design from '78-'82. After graduating I began to pursue a career in comic book illustration. I struggled for five years in NYC, a starving artist trying to make it in the art biz. Finally around '87 I started getting regular work in black and white independent comics. The money sucked, but it was steady work doing what I loved. As my comic book career progressed, I was offered better & better jobs.

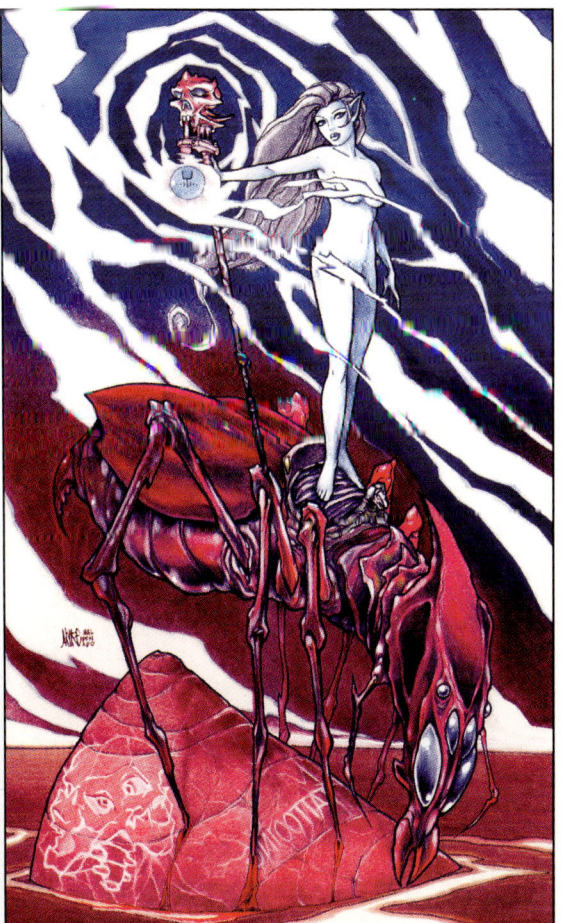

My best achievement in comics came when Kevin Eastman (who now owns this magazine) agreed to publish Flesh Wounds. This full color book was very personal as it dealt with tattooing and piercing, which I'd been into for a couple of years at that point.

As fate would have it in 1990, while illustrating FleshWounds, I was asked to apprentice by Darren Rosa of Rising Dragon in NYC. I accepted and slowly over the next couple of years began tattooing more and illustrating comics less.

As tattooing became my passion, I decided to leave the comic world and devote all my energy to making body art my #1 medium.

I tattooed in Pennsylvania for a few years and traveled around the country attending tattoo conventions before coming back to New York. In early 1999 I joined a group of Tattooers and started All Souls Tattooing in uptown Manhattan.

Wanting to concentrate more on artwork, rather than parlor style tattooing, I have ventured out on my own and begun Dreamland Creations (dreamlandcreations.net). An art studio devoted to custom "one of a kind" art. I'm looking forward to the creations that will come out of Dreamland in the future.

dreamlandcreations.net

Lorenzo Sperlonga was born in Rome in 1969 and at the age of 14, he attended the Italian Institute for Cinematography and Television.

At 17 his career was off and running as he began working for several Italian magazines and advertising agencies as an illustrator and graphic designer. He continued to grow and refine his style for nine years at "Lapis," an advertising agency in Rome, where he created scores of book covers, CD covers, posters, storyboards, and packaging as well as many advertising campaigns.

In 1994, "Skorpio," Italy's largest Comic and Magazine publisher, printed his first "Pin-Up," and Lorenzo decided this was his real calling. Fortunately so did "Skorpio" and the first one led to a series of many, many more. "Lanciostory," "Playboy," and "Penthouse," also start publishing his artwork at this time.

In 1995 he met Kevin Eastman for the first time in Los Angeles. Kevin looked over his portfolio and discussed the possibilities of his working in the American market, and five years later his first cover for Heavy Metal appeared on the newsstands.

Lorenzo lives in Los Angeles, and is now working with a variety of publishers in addition to Heavy Metal. They include "Avalanche Press", "Larry Flynt Publications," "NBM," "Fort Ross," "Linda Jones Enterprises," "Dreamstone" in Australia, "Eura" in Italy and many more.

To see more of his artwork log on www.Metaltv.com or contact him at Spiderello@aol.com

Dorian Cleavenger has achieved world wide acclamation and renown in record time through his unique approach to the Fantasy Art field. With an instantly recognizable style combined with technical proficiency and his infusion of a message into every image through often subtle innuendoes and details, his works, since entering the fantasy area have captured and entranced the art world with a completely new aspect that some have termed "The New School of Fantasy Art".

Recently free lance artist Dorian's original works have had several private and university gallery showings, been published in two books exclusively on his art, several collector card sets, a newly published portfolio of selected paintings, numerous magazine covers and articles featuring his works and he has been doing privately commissioned paintings as well. He shall be attending conventions in Europe this season where he has established a huge fan base.

In his Los Angeles studio Dorian generally creates two or three paintings weekly while employing his favorite medium of acrylics applied by brush on illustration board. Acknowledged by artists as a difficult medium to master, he became adept after a short but intensive trial and error period during which he analyzed and conquered the rapid drying time and color density shifts characteristic of the paint.

About half of Dorian's work is done using models... many well known actresses and entertainers... while the rest are created entirely from his rich and decidedly unconventional imagination. Obviously the female form is his primary inspiration around which he devises a theme to present within a painting as he uses his distinctive talent to create the unusual costuming, props, and lighting, then tying all into an impressive sce-

nario. Incorporating sometimes historical or mythological aspects, transposing time in any direction, not just past, present or future... often with unconventional twists to fantasy art that a few viewers have called "erotically disturbing, yet entrancing and provoking", none can deny his extraordinary challenging of conventional concepts. Dorian's fantasy world relies on a rever-

sal of common perspectives to challenge the viewer. Pulling from his accrued and vast storehouse of mental reference material combined with an incredibly creative and analytical mind, it seems Dorian will not soon run out of material to inspire his paintings.

More images, product availability and information on Dorian can be found on his website: **www.dorianart.com**.

GALLERY

DREW

Bio on Drew
Written by Drew's best friend and writer, Joe Antonelli

Drew's approach to art reflects his attitude toward everything else he does in life. He is on a constant quest for improvement; what he did yesterday is not as good as what he will do today. For Drew, life is a competition and the winners are those who do not give up but continue to pursue their goals to the end.

His talent for art grew quickly, by the age of sixteen he was being paid for his work. But as he was often reminded, art was no way to make a living. He chose to forego college and went to work after high school as a picture framer. Despite his skill as a framer and the clientele he developed, the work was torture for the young artist. Finally, he had to face the inescapable conclusion that art was in his blood and that he would never be satisfied unless he was the one creating.

A move from Seattle to Southern California brought more than a change of weather. He was hired immediately by Image Comics in the Spring of '94 and his work appeared in the comic books of Top Cow, Wildstorm, and Extreme Studios. Working in comics forced Drew to hone his craft. Comics also brought about a change in technique that would not have been possible even a decade earlier: the use of computer airbrush, which allows for greater artistic flexibility and experimentation.

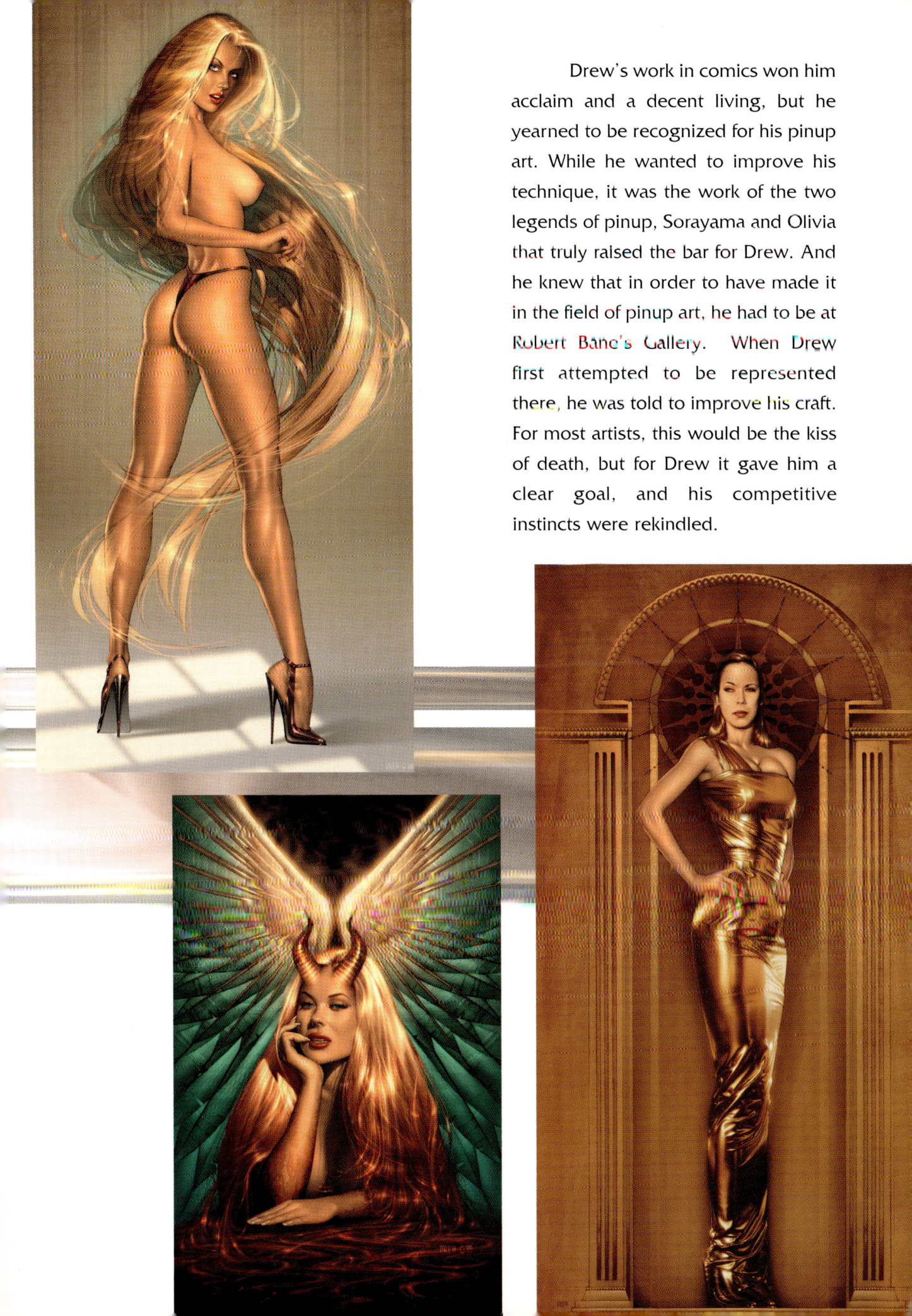

Drew's work in comics won him acclaim and a decent living, but he yearned to be recognized for his pinup art. While he wanted to improve his technique, it was the work of the two legends of pinup, Sorayama and Olivia that truly raised the bar for Drew. And he knew that in order to have made it in the field of pinup art, he had to be at Robert Banc's Gallery. When Drew first attempted to be represented there, he was told to improve his craft. For most artists, this would be the kiss of death, but for Drew it gave him a clear goal, and his competitive instincts were rekindled.

He went back to work, focusing on the details, developing his craft, sacrificing his comfortable living with comics. He was on a mission, one that he could not turn away from without giving up his reason for being. Two years passed, and when he submitted his new work to Bane, he was greeted enthusiastically and welcomed to the gallery.

What you see on these pages reflects his most recent works, and yet these paintings should be viewed as the first phase of a mature artist. These are a precursor to better things to come, as an artist and a person. Drew is still in competition with himself, still experimenting and developing his craft and new ways of expression.

As his career continues, look for Drew's art to bring new perspectives, to transcend where pinup is today, and to continue on his journey of discovery.

You can find more of Drew's work at Robert Bane's gallery site: www.worldofpinup.com
Also, look for his new book at newsstands and bookstores.

BRIAN ROOD

Still a relative newcomer in the industry, Brian Rood is quickly making a name for himself in the illustration field. At only 26, he is currently working on some of the hottest projects in the comics and the entertainment industry.

He has an ongoing relationship with companies such as Dynamic Forces, Chaos! Comics, Image Comics, M/G Publishing and numerous others. Recent accomplishments include lithographs for movie properties such as *Star Trek* and the *Crow*, and his own art book The Art of Brian Rood. This past year has been busier than ever for Brian: producing over a dozen fully painted covers and posters for Chaos! Comics, numerous projects varying from lithograph to cover art for Dynamic Forces, and a fully painted cover for the new *Masters of the Universe* book released by MV Creations and Image Comics. Such accomplishments have certainly confirmed that you will be seeing much more of his work in the near future.

Brian has shown an interest in art all his life. He spent two years of high school in a 3 hour block vocational program studying the commercial art field. From there he attended college studying graphic design. Working odd jobs, designing logos, and running 4 color print presses were good stepping stones but not fulfilling enough for Brian. Once he realized the 9-5 gig wasn't for him, he entered the field of freelance illustration. Long hours and little pay were the norm for the first few years. Brian was still assembling a strong portfolio to show editors and potential

clients. After burning the candle at both ends for a while, all the hard work finally started to pay off. Now he receives frequent phone calls and emails from numerous editors and publishers. The long hours still exist but the results of all his hard work can now be seen throughout his ever-growing list of clients and published work.

Brian's work is a unique blend of acrylic painting, airbrush, color pencil and pastel. He has refined his painting style to rival that of a photograph, yet he maintains an artistic quality that cannot be achieved with a camera lens. You will find that Brian doesn't lock into any one genre of subject matter but rather illustrate all of the things he finds interesting and entertaining. Illustrating the female form is still one of his personal favorites as you will see in his new book The Art of Brian Rood. Brian's book can be found in the collection of art books released through Art Fantastix, MG / Publishing. The

Art of Brian Rood is a collection of his comic art, fantasy art, movie/entertainment art and his most popular female artwork.

Working in the various fields of entertainment art have given Brian the chance to experiment stylistically and grow as an artist with each new project. From photo-realism to Japanimation, all of Brian's projects display the fine craftsmanship that has got him this far this fast. He has proved that with determination, hard work and professionalism, it isn't impossible to succeed in the field of fine art and commercial illustration.

To view more of Brian's work please go to www.brianrood.com and be sure to pick up The Art of Brian Rood at bookstores and newsstands everywhere

GALLERY
Scott Burton's Universe

Scott Burton's paintings, prints, films, and sculptures have not only appeared in various exhibitions and galleries over the past twelve years, but on covers, in articles and in books including *Spectrum: The Best in Contemporary Fantastic Art*. His works are owned by many well-known artists and art collectors.

Currently, Scott produces miniatures, models, paintings and sculptures for feature films and commercials. For the past few years, he has worked primarily with legendary Star Wars special effects model maker Grant McCune on many films and commercials. Most recently, Scott has contributed to Red Planet, Clockstoppers, Spiderman, Minority Report, The Core, and the upcoming sequel to X-Men.

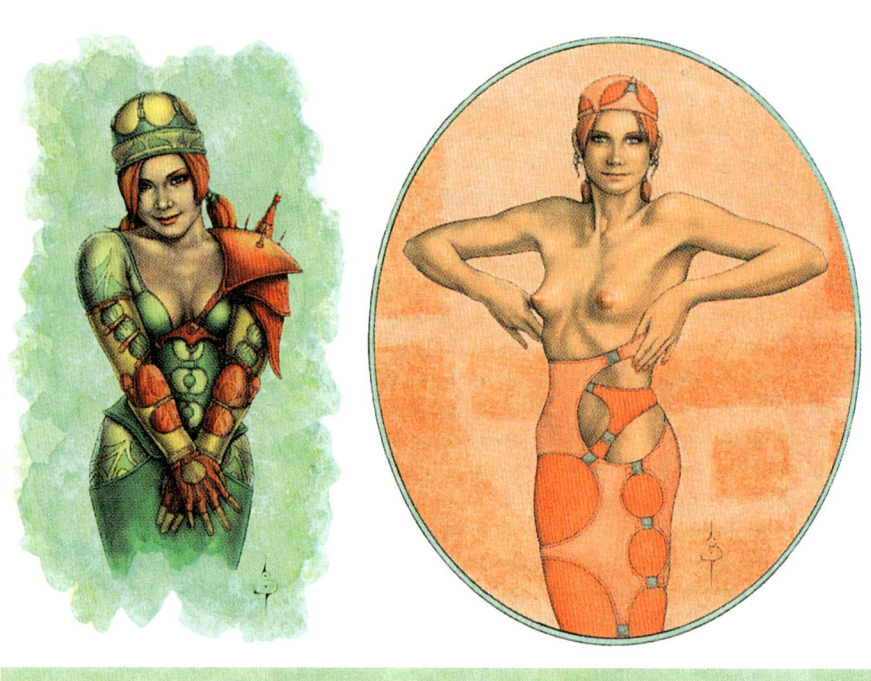

Future projects include an art book of Scott's personal work and a remake of his animated student film This is My Shadow. He is also in the early stages of a very ambitious illustrated novel featuring his own words and paintings.

Scott Burton can be contacted by email at sbuniverse@tcsn.net

Ciruelo Cabral was born in Buenos Aires, Argentina on July 20, 1963. His formal art training was limited to a few courses in drawing and advertising design, after which, at the age of 18, he immediately found work in an ad agency as an illustrator. At 21 Ciruelo became a freelance illustrator and has not looked back since.

Sketch from "Magia, The Ciruelo Sketchbook" published by SQP

Courtesy of Lucasfilm Ltd. ©Lucasfilm Ltd. & TM. All rights reserved. Used under authorization. Unauthorized duplication is a violation of applicable law.

In 1987 Ciruelo traveled to Europe and settled in Sitges, a small town near Barcelona, Spain. He then embarked on a search for publishers for his "worlds of fantasy", eventually finding them in Spain, England, the United States, and Germany. Ciruelo continues to work for U.S. publishers, among them, Bantam for whom he did book covers for the trilogy, "Chronicles of the Shadow War" by George Lucas. Other clients include Wizards of the Coast (Magic cards), TSR, Berkley, Tor, Warner, Ballantine, Heavy Metal, and Playboy. Cabral also has created a number of rock album covers, Steve Vai being one of them.

Sketch from "Magia, The Ciruelo Sketchbook" published by SQP

Cover image from "Magia, The Ciruelo Sketchbook" published by SQP

In 1997 the book, Luz, the Art of Ciruelo was published. This book features over 160 full color illustrations and a number of pencil sketches laid out in 128 pages. In the year 2000, Magia, the Ciruelo Sketchbook was published by SQP Inc.

In 1998 Ciruelo and his wife, Daniela founded DAC Editions which controls all the copyrights of his artbooks. They are also producing posters and CD-Roms featuring Ciruelo's artwork.

To find out more about Ciruelo Cabral and to view some of his artwork, log on to:
www.dac-editions.com

III MILLENNIUM - MEMORY
GREY OVER A GREYER GREY

22nd December 2058

I remember thousands of apocalyptic stories that were written in the last half of that twentieth century of my youth. There was also a variety of versions; the Third World War, a nuclear war, radioactive leaks, and i don't know what else.
The saddest thing is that such a long time has elapsed and i still don't know what happened. It is true that this century is bewildering, it is true that part of the XXth century civilization has disappeared, but as usually happens, nobody knows why.
We are always caressed or wounded by the horizon, whatever year it may be.
I have seen the sweetness once again. A sweetness made of circuits and optic fibre.
I have seen the horror of grey cold serve as heat.

LIAM SHARP

Liam Sharp describes his work as "lovingly eclectic". He has created artwork for a wide range of titles with an equally diverse readership, from the hub of the mainstream to the boundaries of cultism.

Titles that Liam has worked on include *Judge Dredd* and the *ABC Warriors* for Fleetway, *Death's Head 2, Spiderman, Venom, The Hulk, XMen*, and the *Manthing* for Marvel, Frank Frazetta's *Death Dealer, Jaguar God* and *G.O.T.H.* for Verotik, *Spawn: The Dark Ages* for Todd McFarlane Productions, and various Batman and Superman titles for DC Comics.

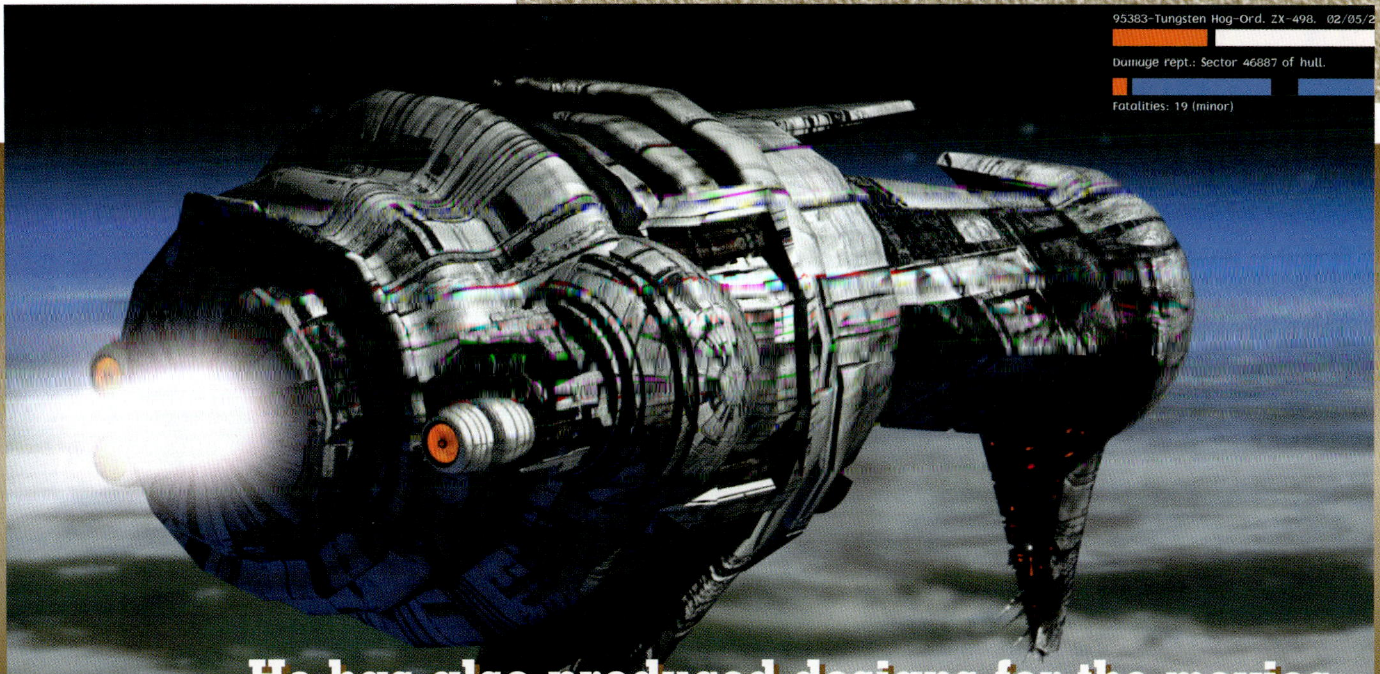

95383-Tungsten Hog-Ord. ZX-498. 02/05/2
Damage rept.: Sector 46887 of hull.
Fatalities: 19 (minor)

He has also produced designs for the movies, "Lost in Space" and "Toy Soldiers" and for the animated TV series, "Batman Beyond".

Liam is currently involved in a creator owned project called, "The Wayfarer's Gem" from which the bulk of this artwork is taken.

Happily married to Christina, Liam has two children, Matylda and Lorcan. He lives and works in Derby, right in the heart of the English midlands.

GALLERY

Ken Kelly

· DEMON OF THE DEEP ·

STRANGE AND STRONG, THE ART OF KEN KELLY SPEAKS TO THE VIEWER JUST AS HE MIGHT. STRAIGHTFORWARD, YET WITH A HINT OF HUMOR IN ITS VOICE. WHILE THE ART DRAWS US IN AND MAKES US NOTICE EVERY BRILLIANT, MOODY DETAIL, THE ARTIST LIGHTHEARTEDLY SCOLDS: "DON'T TAKE IT SO SERIOUSLY!"

AFTER A TOUR OF DUTY IN THE MILITARY, KELLY SETTLED BACK IN NEW YORK. INFLUENCED BY A NUMBER OF ARTISTS' WORK IN THE FANTASY AND SCIENCE FICTION GENRES, KEN DECIDED TO MAKE A GO OF AN ILLUSTRATION CAREER. IN 1968 HIS FIRST COMMISSIONED PAINTING, "THE LURKING TERROR" WAS PUBLISHED ON THE COVER OF VAMPIRELLA MAGAZINE.

THE NEXT 29 YEARS WOULD PROVE TO BE A ROLLER COASTER RIDE OF HARD WORK AND SUCCESS FOR KEN. HE'S ILLUSTRATED MORE THAN 200 MAGAZINE COVERS, ONE OF WHICH CAUGHT THE EYES OF THE ROCK BAND KISS AND LED TO HIS ILLUSTRATION OF THEIR ALBUMS "DESTROYER" AND "LOVE GUN". HIS WORK WITH KISS EARNED HIM TWO GOLD ALBUMS, AND OPENED THE DOOR TO SIMILAR PROJECTS WITH BANDS LIKE DEEP PURPLE AND MOST CURRENTLY MANOWAR.

· TIGRESS ·

· SCALED VENGEANCE ·

• DEATH'S END •

• "THE KEEPER" •

PAPERBACK BOOK COVER ILLUSTRATION HAS ALSO BEEN A CORNERSTONE OF KEN'S CAREER; EARLY ON HE ESTABLISHED HIMSELF AS THE COVER ARTIST FOR THE ROBERT E. HOWARD "CONAN" SERIES. HE DID MANY OTHER PAPERBACK COVERS, BUT IT IS HIS ASSOCIATION WITH CONAN THAT BECAME ONE OF HIS MOST ENDURING. IN FACT, IT QUALIFIED HIM AS SUCH A CONAN EXPERT THAT HE WAS ASKED TO SERVE AS VISUAL CONSULTANT FOR THE NEW FILM "KULL THE CONQUEROR."

KEN'S ART HAS GRACED TOY PACKAGES FROM THE TRANSFORMERS TO G.I. JOE AND, THANKS TO A NUMBER OF LUCRATIVE TEXTILE LICENSING DEALS INVOLVING KEN'S TRANSFORMERS ART, HIS YOUNGEST FANS CAN LITERALLY SLEEP ON IT! SPEAKING OF FANS, KEN'S ARE AMONG THE GENRE'S MOST LOYAL, AND IT WAS IN RESPONSE TO THEIR OVERWHELMING DEMAND THAT KEN'S BOOK, "THE ART OF KEN KELLY" WAS PUBLISHED IN 1990. ADD TO THAT KEN'S MOST RECENT WORK IN THE TRADING CARD AND COMIC BOOK ARENAS, AND IT'S EASY TO SEE WHY KEN'S RENOWNED AS ONE OF FANTASY'S HARDEST WORKING, MOST DIVERSE AND MOST TALENTED ARTISTS.

· SOLITAIRE ·

AS FOR THE HARD WORKING PART, KEN WOULDN'T HAVE IT ANY OTHER WAY. HIS MOTTO: "I'M LUCKY TO BE ABLE TO DO WHAT I LOVE AND MAKE A LIVING AT IT, SO I'LL KEEP DOING IT AS LONG AS THEY'LL LET ME!"

THE BOOK YOU HAVE BEEN WAITING FOR.....
KEN KELLYS *ESCAPE* NOW ON SALE!
www.KenKellyArt.com

Please send check or Money order to;
KELLY PRINTS INC.
179 San Juan Drive
Hauppauge, New York 11788

Name
Address
City   State   Zip
Phone Number (with area code)
E-mail Address

Hard Cover $34.95 , Soft Cover $24.95   postage included
Or order online at, www.kenkellyart.com

Marc soon revealed the extent of his brimming imagination, but he was careful to seek out his masters among the great artists of the past - Velazquez, Degas and Caravaggio - as well as among the artists published in the legendary, but now defunct, French comics magazine "Pilote". A quick learner, he sketched regularly from life and everyday situations which he found to be the best way of creating interesting characters. Unfortunately, his passion for art undermined his academic career and he just barely managed to scrape through his high school graduation.

Obviously, his countless sketches were not putting the food on the table and our budding artist had to try his hand at a variety of jobs and professions. He used his experiences to strengthen the links between day-to-day reality and his abundant imagination.

In 1998, he switched to the world of video games and suddenly found himself laughing all the way to the bank. To his own words, this "act of betrayal" to his first love, besides allowing him to eat three square meals a day, has also enabled him to develop his knowledge of techniques other than the traditional ones of clay and copper-plate engraving. At a book-signing he met Corbeyran and the two creators hit it off immediately. Their first collaboration - interspersed with numerous meals and much hearty laughter - resulted in an illustration for the special issue called "Stryges, Myths and Reality."

Soon after, their joint talents produced the "Regulator" series which recounts the tormented adventures of a hit man, torn between his love life and the cold-bloodedness of his profession.

You ain't seen the last of them yet!

Carlos Diez

Carlos Diez is one of the most famous artists of pin-ups in Spain. Always in love with mythical Betty Page and Marilyn Monroe drawings, he now resurrects the genre his own way with the girls of his dreams.

Diez was born in Madrid, Spain on October 16, 1966. After finishing his required education, he decided to begin his artistic studies at the University of Fine Arts and the School of Applied Arts but he quit after a year because of his restless creativity and the incapacity of such institutions in dealing with it.

Self-teaching and his skills with the technique of airbrushing helped him to start publishing his first works for record labels and advertising agencies in the late 1980's. During this period he also started teaching illustration and drawing.

His restless spirit for art took him down the road that would drive him toward his favorite inspiration: female curves and fantasy. From this came his well-known pin-ups and erotic portraits of famous women, which have brought him broad popularity because of his incredible realism and above all, because of the way he combines his models' personalities with his own fantasies.

His illustrations can be seen in posters and magazine covers all over the world in such publications as Kiss Comics, El Vibora, Eros Comics, Gigamesh, Dolmen, Heavy Metal, Playboy, Penthouse, GQ and much more.

Carlos Diez is now preparing for the upcoming release of his first illustrated book along with a leading role in the education center he founded.

LAWRENCE NORTHEY

Most of what Lawrence Northey does in sculpture comes from just doing it and by staying interested in a lot of seemingly different things. As an example, he reflects on his love of custom motor-cycles and hot rods.

"Razor"- 1996, Height- 25 inches
One of several machines believed to have been a competitor in the Ball Game. This one was discovered in a subterranean chamber of the Cenote di Xtoloc, Chichen Itza.

"Quetzalcoatl & Her Entourage"- 1999
Height- 36 inches
The Ruler of Wired City shown here with the Royal Guard.

"I'm consistently dazzled by the level of artistry by people like Arlen Ness and the late Big Daddy Roth," claims Northey. "Science Fiction in comics and movies have also influenced me a great deal, as have the works of the surrealists in the thirties and forties. I'm really all over the place when it comes to where I get my ideas. I like to combine all these different interests and sculpt what appears to have come from some parallel universe's Museum of Antiquities."

"Chantecler Eldorado"- 1998, Height- 28 inches
As the Gamemaster he would drop from the sky on a shining silver board tossing the "pelota", or ball, signaling the beginning of the Ball Game.

"USA-STAR 1"- 2001
Height- 38 inches
A Sentient Terrain Autonomous Robot designed to replace a human pilot in the cockpit of a spacecraft destined for Mars in the year 2025

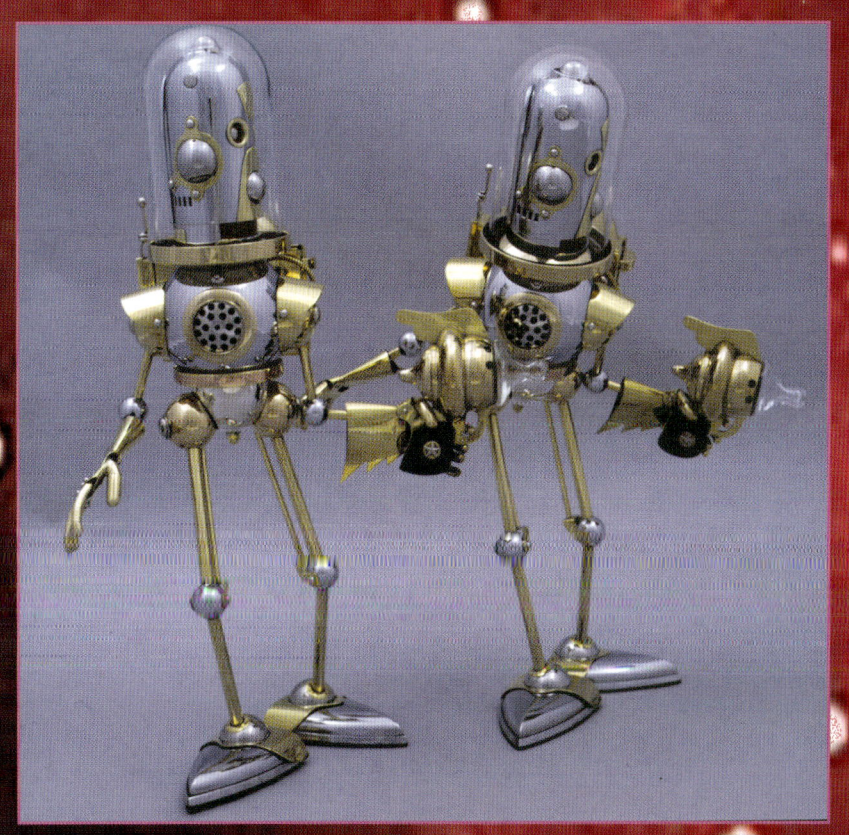

"Star Pirates"- 2001
Height- 27 inches
Linked to the Battle of Calakmul and the Search for the Interface (scholars generally agree this battle signaled the end of the robot society).

"L-ROY"- 2001
Height- 20 inches
Special Assistant to USA-STAR 1 on the ill-fated mission to Mars.

"Spaceman Troy"- 1998
Height- 23 inches
An early GSA (Global Space Agency) prototype for the mission to Mars.

Northey explains that his creative process usually sparks with an idea that he feels would be fun to make. Then, quite naturally, a story evolves. He sees the characters freeze framed in a moment, like a still taken from a movie. He insists that he quite literally watches the movie in his mind and then chooses the frame he thinks would be the most interesting to develop three dimensionally.

"Joolie Ginseng"- 2002
Height- 28 inches
A denizen of Wired City she was discovered near Chantecler Eldorado, implying a possible link between the two.

"OTTOmatic #9"- 2002
Height- 24 inches
Several of these have been unearthed near Chichen Itza suggesting they were part of some common work force.

A story he's titled, "Wired City" has evolved from this method of creating. Working with his wife, script writer Julie Northey and illustrator Anil Sharma, "Wired City" is taking shape as a graphic novel.

Northey works in metal and often fiberglass. He does commissions and speculative work exclusively. His work is collected internationally. Sculptures, including works currently available to collectors, may be viewed on his website at www.robotart.net

Jason Freeny

Jason Freeny has been a New York City artist for more than a decade. Originally from the Washington DC metro area, Jason attended the Pratt Institute to study Industrial Design, and remained in Brooklyn for 6 years after college. After college, he worked at a Tribeca mural company as a painter. The job entailed plenty of travel, as the murals were installed and painted around the world.

These jobs were massive, with some lasting for as long as three months. It was in Germany on one of these protracted trips (or, as Jason puts it "while I was stranded in Oberhausen...") that Jason first became interested in pin-up art, and started drawing his own. At first, these figures were just pretty girls artfully posed, simple cheesecake. He used pastels, and the figures had a pleasing softness to them.

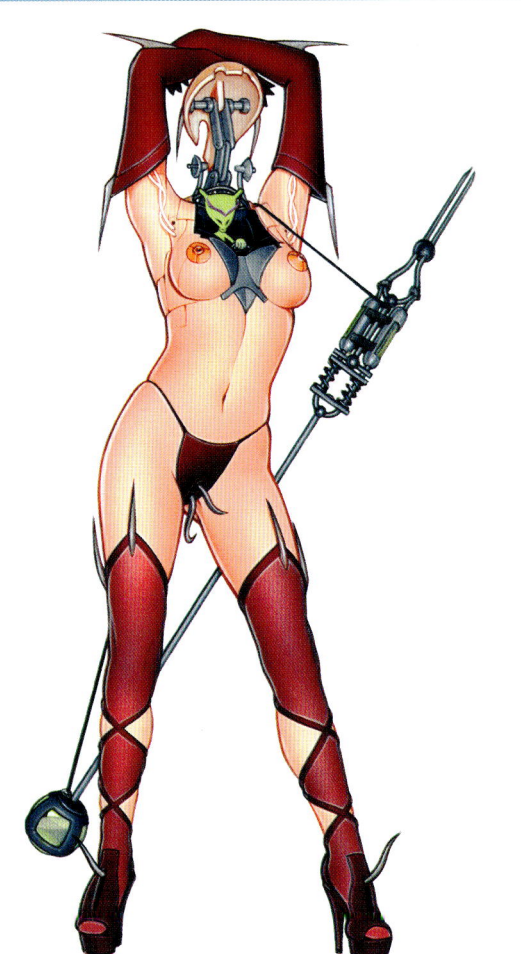
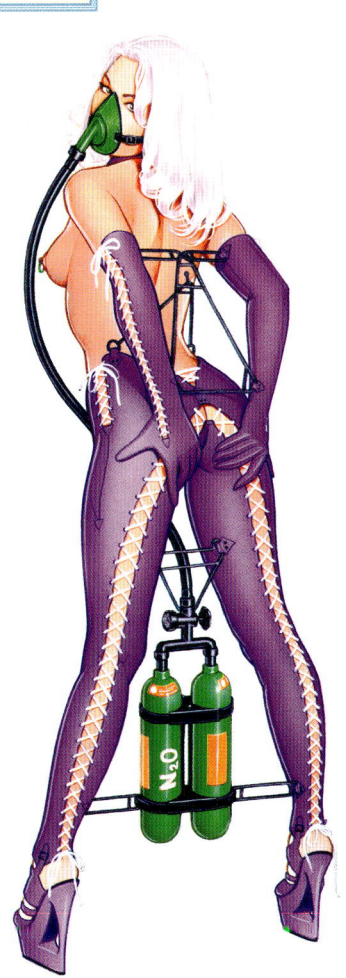
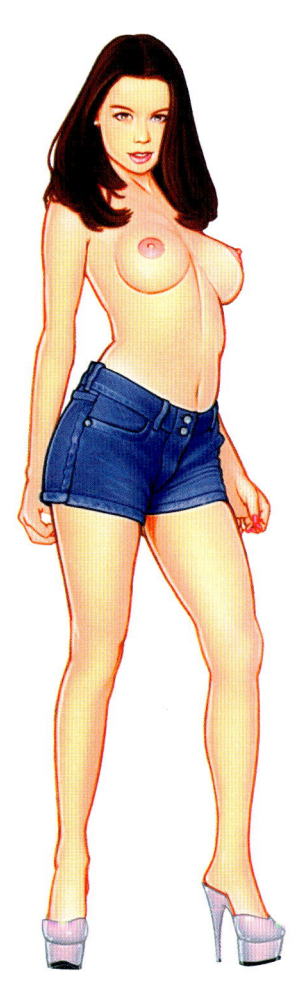

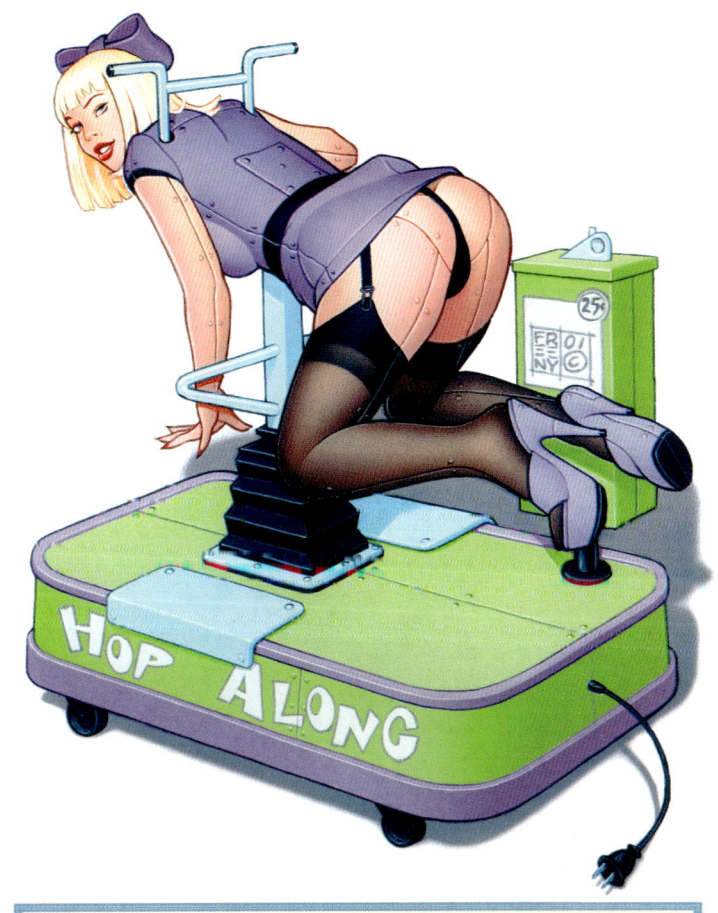

After leaving the mural company, he continued with his pin-up work, further refining his figures, and settling on airbrushed acrylic as his chosen medium, giving his figures a hardness, an edge that they had lacked previously. For the next four years, Jason worked at MTV as a freelance designer, utilizing his industrial design for background creating sets and props for various MTV events. His pinups were beginning to take on an industrial look as well.

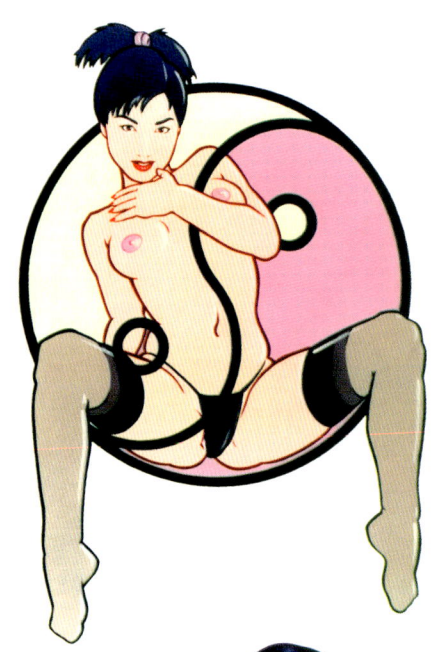

no longer satisfied with just the female figure, jason's paintings began to take on a fetishistic cast as he experimented with different forms. jason's illustrations can be seen in several penthouse's publications, most notably the mascot used in asian fever magazine. currently working as a designer at a toy company, jason now resides in manhattan with his wife and infant son. for work inquiries, contact freenydesign@nyc.rr.com

FELIX VEGA

Felix Vega was born in Santiago de Chile in 1971. His first works appeared in Chilean, Argentinean and Japanese publications; at the same time he studied art and worked for audiovisual producers, animation studios and advertising agencies.

Between 1994 and 2002 he made a series of short stories, with scripts by Enrique Abuli, for the Spanish edition of Playboy. Some of these stories form part of the "Playboy comics", "Trios", and "Femmes Fatales".

In 1996 he published the first part of his four-part work "Juan Buscamares" - "Water". This would later be published in France, Spain, Holland, Germany, Italy, Brazil and the USA in the pages of Heavy Metal Magazine. "Water" was followed by "Air", "Earth" and "Fire", which completes the series of the saga. He also made a short film based on the fantastic universe of "Juan Buscamares".

Vega has contributed to French, Italian and Spanish magazines. He has exhibited in Japan, Spain, Andorra and Chile. His work as an illustrator has won him prizes both in Chile and Spain.

He currently lives in Barcelona.

KEN MEYER JR.

Ken Meyer Jr. has worked as an illustrator/designer for close to 20 years. He has worked in comics (being nominated for an Eisner award in the process), paper games (Magic the Gathering, White Wolf games and many more), online games (the popular Everquest) and more.

He has also worked in the education industry, in professional training, web design and other areas. Among his stranger jobs was working 'across the field from Area 51,' on the Stealth Fighter when it was still classified.

Current projects include the Tori Amos RAINN benefit calendar (05/06), which he designed, produced and did a painting for, along with work for Bell Helmets and many private commissions. He has lived in more than 10 states, the Philippines, and now resides in his old junior high school haunt, Savannah, Georgia. More work can be seen on his site at www.kenmeyerjr.com and he can be reached at kenmeyerjr@coastalnow.net

Paluzzi

... It's a question that has plagued mankind like a festering virus since the invention of speech, When we crawled out from caves and thoughts formed the first sentences in order for the masses to communicate, saying such things as, "Raw meat too chewy", and "Owww... Fire is freakin' hot!"
Stuff like that.
Actually the question that pops up most is, "What the hell are you doing?"... The people who tend to ask this are those that didn't know me when I was younger. When I took two fake severed heads made from Styrofoam and had them painted the color of Caucasian flesh, cut the top off one so it appeared scalped, spreading lots of dry fake blood I mixed on the severed section, and took the other head and dripped blood from it's gouged out eye sockets. A noose made from shoestring rope went around both of their necks, and then I hung them from my bedroom window... on the outside. I guess being the only white kid growing up in Eastchester Housing Projects in the Bronx wasn't enough to get attention. I had to make the neighborhood think I was insane as well. Was there something seriously wrong with me?
You bet.

Most artists point to other artists as their inspiration. People who laid paint brush to canvas, creating something vivid and striking. I point to movies and music. At eleven years of age I discovered the most visual band in history, KISS, and I was taken, overwhelmed. From that moment on something had to assault my eyes to get my attention, or it had to blend well, or it had to at least damn well look good! And of course The Rocky Horror Picture Show was a must. So when I started doing the art I came at it from a different direction, developing a style before learning the process or the technique. It was not like learning how to walk before learning how to crawl, but it was like writing a novel in the 1st grade while learning to spell. Fortunately I learned how to spell shortly before September 11th. The original photograph was taken in the morning on an early spring day. The picture is of the South side of the South Tower. Two days after the attack I opened the scan of the shot. They say artists speak through their work, and for me this image is my raging scream. WE WILL NEVER FORGET. It's an expression that has been used countless times since, because we all felt its sentiment together. It became our battle cry. This particular piece has easily become my most recognizable work, appearing in an exhibit along side the likes of Peter Max at the George Bush Presidential Library and Museum. It has been given to victims and the workers who risked their lives in both the retrieval and the cleanup after the attack, and it has been used to raise funds in charity events.

Now if only I always used my powers for good.

But some other things are just fun to do. Who doesn't want eyes almost as large as their head, or appendages where there should be none? I like my entertainment in my face where I can see it because it's pushing itself into my eyes, squeezing to fit through my pupils. I'm not happy until my optic nerves jump because my retinas have been assaulted, my frontal lobes are reeling and the rest of my brain is firing charges through its synaptic nerves, sending bolts of electricity down my spine.

I'm inspired by the visual. Coffee in a tan mug, puckering red lips under a black star, the sight of dimension, and the view of the screen closing in while you're blacking out.

Stuff like that.

Look for Anthony's upcoming novel, REVOLUTION.

The work of PALUZZI can be found at: http//paluzzi.net

EDGAR ESPINO

Born in 1977, Edgar Espino began his freelance practice in early 1995. A self-taught artist, his ability to portray the female form in various settings has made him one of the best illustrators of erotic-fantasy art in Chicago.

His art has been shown in various private exhibitions and shows with great success, regardless of the opinion of critics who's input have only contributed to the artist's sympathy among peers and fans of his work. His paintings show a personal admiration for the female spirit through pin-up, fantasy and erotic images. A trademark like that of the artists he admires.

Over the past few years his development as an artist has progressed along with his fascination for female sensuality. Following the steps of other great artists such as Carlos Cartagena and Lorenzo Sperlonga to name a few, his expression of thought is becoming a nice addition to the modern world of pin ups and erotic fantasy art.

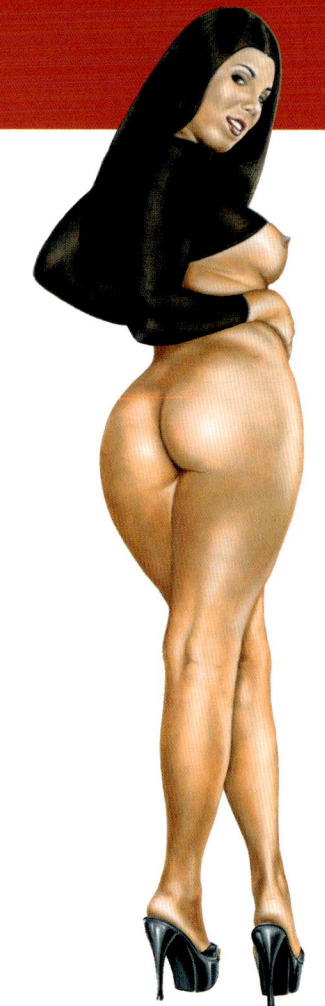

VICTORIA FRANCIS

Victoria Frances was born on October 25, 1982. Early on, she was fascinated by the Galizan woods (in Northwestern Spain) which is where she spent her childhood.

Victoria was captived by the gothic atmospheres of towns like Paris and London, where legendary novels of the gothic genre took place. Her illustrations and sketches represent some of this genre.

At present she continues her studies of Fine Arts in Valencia while continue to illustrate book covers and other commissioned works. *FAVOLE,* her first illustrated book is a remembrance through the towns of Verona, Venecia, and Genova, where she links the illustrations to a story of a desolate atmosphere and extrem melancholy.